CLASSICS *Illustrated®* **Deluxe**

The Adventures of TOM SAWYER

BY MARK TWAIN

ADAPTED BY JEAN DAVID MORVAN, FREDERIQUE VOULYZE AND SEVERINE LEFEBVRE

PAPERCUT Z

CLASSICS ILLUSTRATED GRAPHIC NOVELS AVAILABLE FROM PAPERCUTZ

CLASSICS ILLUSTRATED DELUXE:

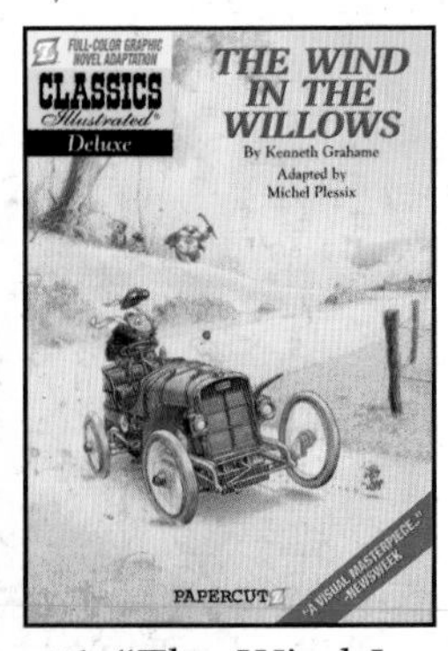

#1 "The Wind In The Willows"

#2 "Tales From The Brothers Grimm"

#3 "Frankenstein"

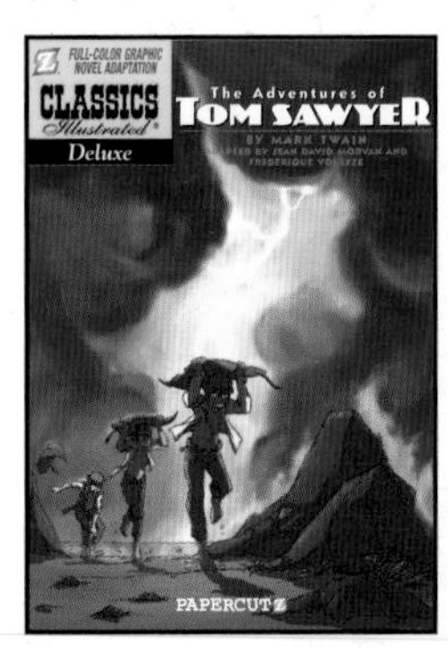

#4 "The Adventures of Tom Sawyer"

CLASSICS ILLUSTRATED:

#1 "Great Expectations"

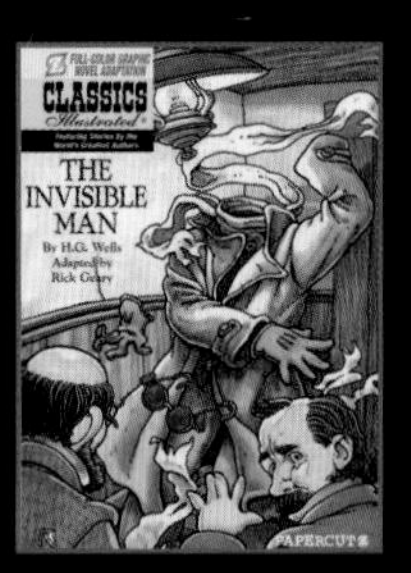

#2 "The Invisible Man"

#3 "Through the Looking-Glass"

#4 "The Raven and Other Poems"

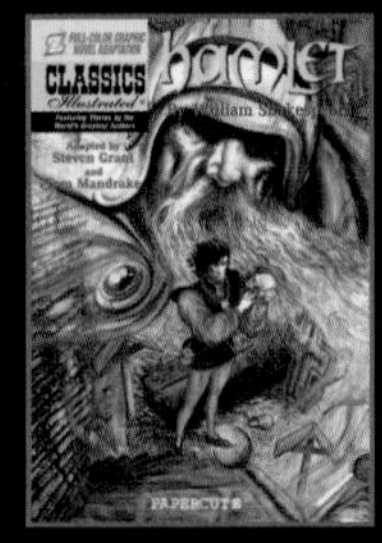

#5 "Hamlet"

#6 "The Scarlet Letter"

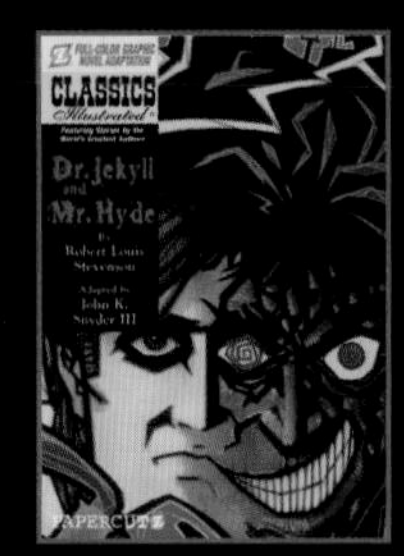

Coming December '09
#7 "Dr. Jekyll and Mr. Hyde"

Classics Illustrated Deluxe are available for $13.95 each in paperback and $17.95 in hardcover. Classics Illustrated are available only in hardcover for $9.95 each. Please add $4.00 for postage and handling for the first book, add $1.00 for each additional book. MC, Visa, Amex accepted or make check payable to NBM Publishing.

Send to: **Papercutz, 40 Exchange Place, Suite 1308, New York, NY 10005 • 1-800-866-1223**

WWW.PAPERCUTZ.COM

The Adventures of TOM SAWYER

BY MARK TWAIN
ADAPTED BY JEAN DAVID MORVAN, FREDERIQUE VOULYZE
AND SEVERINE LEFEBVRE

PAPERCUTZ™
New York

Thanks to Claudio who does a good job as the artist's spouse!
To my parents, to Jean David and Frédérique and everyone at 510 TTC,
To the whole Delcourt team,
To Diane and to the Loup,
To Steph and Vince.
Thank you, Véro, for the lessons,
And to Rammstein for their daily support.
S. L.

To Mamoune.
Domo arigato, Corazonchan, for the shared adventures.
F. V.

I was very taken with the cartoon adaptation of Tom Sawyer *when I was 10 years old, and then by Mark Twain's novel. I'd never imagined drawing my own* Tom Sawyer *one day! The principal difficulty lay in the necessity, from a graphics standpoint, of getting detached from the character's image in the cartoon in order to make him my own. It was difficult at first, but you have to get into your characters' skin, to absorb the story into yourself, and let the magic of drawing take place—*
Séverine Lefèbvre

The Adventures of Tom Sawyer
By Mark Twain
Adapted by Jean David Morvan, Frédérique Voulyzé and Séverine Lefèbvre

Translation by Joe Johnson
Lettering by Ortho
John Haufe and William B. Jones Jr. — Classics Illustrated Historians
Michael Petranek — Editorial Assistant
Jim Salicrup
Editor-in-Chief

ISBN: 978-1-59707-153-6 paperback edition
ISBN: 978-1-59707-152-9 hardcover edition

Printed in China.
Regent Printing
6/F Hang Tung Resource Centre No. 18
A Kung Ngam Village Road
Shau Kei Wan, Hong Kong

Distributed by Macmillan.

10 9 8 7 6 5 4 3 2 1

TOM?!

TO-OM!!

IF I EVER CATCH YOU.

>PFF<
>PFF<
I'D HAVE SWORN HE WAS HIDING IN THERE.

I NEVER DID SEE THE BEAT OF THAT BOY!

I'VE GOT YOU, RASCAL!!

BUT I WEREN'T HIDING, AUNT POLLY!

OH YES, THEN WHAT HAVE YOU BEEN UP TO IN THE ARMOIRE?
'SPECIALLY WITH YOUR HANDS AND MOUTH COVERED WITH JAM I TOLD YOU NOT TO TOUCH!

THAT--JAM? WELL, THAT REALLY AIN'T LIKE ME--

AND WHAT'S THIS THEN?
UH, WELL, UH--

LOOK OUT BEHIND YOU!!!

AAA!!

HANG THE BOY!

CAN'T I NEVER LEARN ANYTHING?
I SHOULD EXPECT ANYTHING COMING FROM HIM.

HE EVEN KNOWS HOW TO MAKE ME LAUGH WHEN I GET MY DANDER UP, THEN IT'S ALL DOWN AGAIN. I AIN'T DOING MY DUTY BY THAT BOY, AND THAT'S THE LORD'S TRUTH, GOODNESS KNOWS.

BUT LAWS-A-ME! HE'S MY OWN DEAD SISTER'S BOY, AND I AIN'T GOT THE HEART TO LASH HIM.

EVERY TIME I LET HIM OFF, MY CON-SCIENCES DOES HURT ME SO.

AND EVERY TIME I HIT HIM MY OLD HEART MOST BREAKS.

"I HOPE AT LEAST HE WON'T BE OFF PLAYING HOOKY."

HA HA! HOW I SLIPPED RIGHT THROUGH HER FINGERS! AUNT POLLY MUST BE AWFUL MAD AT ME.
LUCKY SHE LOVES ME TOO MUCH TO BE SPITEFUL.
I'D EVEN RECKON SHE THOUGHT I WENT TO SCHOOL.

TO TELL THE TRUTH, I DID HEAD THAT WAY, AT FIRST. AND THEN I GOT SIDETRACKED TO GO SHAKE HANDS WITH HUCK.

WE RACED THROUGH THE TREES --
AND THEN, ONCE WE PASSED OVER THE MISSISSIPPI --WE COULDN'T RESIST.

WHILE WE WAS DRYING IN THE SUN, I PONDERED ON MY POOR FRIENDS FIGURING OUT MATH PROBLEMS ABOUT TWO BODIES DUNKED INTO WATER--

--OR WORKING ON MY SPELLING LISTS.

SPEAKING OF WORK, TOM, COULDN'T YOU GIVE US A HAND WITH THIS?
NO -- SORRY -- NO WAY. IT'S NIGH ON TIME FOR SUPPER. IF I WAS TO GET DIRTY, I WON'T HAVE TIME TO WASH UP.

IT DON'T NO MATTER TO YOU! YOU'RE ALREADY IN YOUR WORK CLOTHES!

TOM, IT WAS MID-DLING WARM IN SCHOOL, WARN'T IT?
YES'M.
POWER-FUL WARM?
YES'M.
DIDN'T YOU WANT TO GO IN A-SWIMMING, TOM?
NO'M-- WELL, NOT VERY MUCH.
SOME OF US PUMPED ON OUR HEADS-- MINE'S DAMP YET. SEE?
THAT SOUNDS TRUE ENOUGH, YOUR SHIRT'S DRY.

THE OTHER BOYS TOOK OFF THEIR SHIRTS, BUT I HAD TO BE CAREFUL, BECAUSE YOU'D SEWED UP THE COLLAR!
I'M SORRY. I FIGURED YOU'D PLAYED HOOKY AND HAD GONE TO THE RIVER.
I RECKON YOU'RE A KIND OF SINGED CAT, AS THE SAYING IS--BETTER'N YOU LOOK.

EXCUSE ME, AUNT, BUT--
--THIS MORNING, I THOUGHT YOU SEWED TOM'S COLLAR--
--WITH WHITE THREAD.
AND THIS ONE IS BLACK!!!!

THE SCOUNDREL!

TOM!!

SID, YOU'LL PAY FOR THAT!!

YOU'VE GOTTA COME OUT SOONER OR LATER!
AND YOU'VE GOT A LICKING A-COMING!

DANG IT!

SOMETIMES SHE SEWS IT WITH WHITE, AND SOMETIMES SHE SEWS IT WITH BLACK.
I WISH SHE'D STICK TO ONE OR T'OTHER--I CAN'T KEEP THE RUN OF 'EM.

SHE'D NEVER NOTICED IF IT HADN'T BEEN FOR SID.

I'LL LEARN HIM!

YOU ASKED FOR IT!!

I CAN LICK YOU!
I'D LIKE TO SEE YOU TRY IT!

I DON'T LIKE CITY SLICKERS.
I HATE HICKS.
IF YOU SAY MUCH I'LL--
MUCH-- MUCH--*MUCH*. THERE NOW!

'MIGHTY SMART, AREN'T YOU? I COULD LICK YOU WITH ONE HAND TIED BEHIND ME, IF I WANTED TO.

YOU *SAY* YOU CAN DO IT. I'VE SEEN WHOLE FAMILIES IN THE SAME FIX.
AND NEVER SOMEONE SO RIDICULOUS IN A HAT.

IF YOU GIVE ME MUCH MORE OF YOUR SASS, I'LL TAKE AND BOUNCE A ROCK OFF'N YOUR HEAD!
I DARE YOU TO KNOCK IT OFF--AND ANY-BODY THAT'LL TAKE A DARE WILL SUCK EGGS.
YOU'RE SAYING YOU WILL BECAUSE YOU'RE AFRAID.

I *AIN'T* AFRAID.
YOU ARE.
I AIN'T.
YOU ARE.

I DARE YOU TO STEP OVER THAT.

NOW YOU SAID YOU'D DO IT, NOW LET'S SEE YOU DO IT.
COME ON.
FOR TWO CENTS I *WILL* DO IT.

HOLLER 'NUFF!

NEVER!!

HOLLER 'NUFF!

'NUFF--

NOW THAT'LL LEARN YOU. BETTER LOOK OUT WHO YOU'RE FOOLING WITH NEXT TIME.

COWARD!

I FOUGHT GOOD, BUT I FIGURE MY WORST HURTING'S STILL TO COME.

OWW! OUCH!!

THIRTY YARDS--

I DON'T SEE WHAT GOOD LIFE IS IF'N YOU SPEND ALL YOUR TIME WORKING.

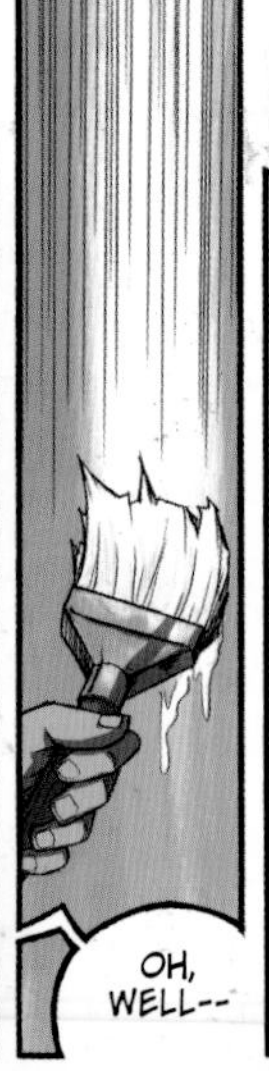
OH, WELL--

AND ONE!

MORE THAN--

>PFF<. I AIN'T EVEN LEARNED HOW TO COUNT AS MANY AS I'VE GOT LEFT.

I'D BE BETTER OFF AT SCHOOL, DON'T YOU KNOW.

SAY, JIM, I'LL FETCH THE WATER IF YOU'LL WHITEWASH SOME.
CAN'T LET YOU GO IN MY PLACE AND ME DO YOUR WHITEWASHIN'.

IF YOU AGREE, I'LL GIVE YOU THIS WHITE MARBLE.

OLE MISSIS SAY SHE SPEC' MARSE TOM GWINE TO AX ME TO WHITEWASH, AN' SO SHE TOLE ME TO SAY NO, 'CAUSE YOU'D BE HAVING FUN WITH THOSE FOLKS HANGING OUT THERE ALL DA TIME, QUARRELIN' AND SKYLARKIN'.

ALL RIGHT, BUT YOU COME BACK QUICK, 'PROMISE?

PROM--

OWW!! OUCH!

AND I'D BETTER NOT CATCH YOU AGAIN.

ALL I NEEDED WAS THAT CUR BEN ROGERS.
BUT-- IF I--
HELLO, OLD CHAP, YOU GOT TO WORK, HEY?
I'LL THINK ABOUT YOU WHILE I'M A-SWIMMING.
AND I'LL BE SORRY FOR YOU DOING THE SAME THING EVERY SATURDAY WHILE I'M HAVING FUN WHITEWASHING.

OH, COME NOW, YOU DON'T MEAN TO LET ON THAT YOU *LIKE* IT?
YOU GET ON DOWN TO THE RIVER, YOU'RE RUINING MY FUN.

SAY, TOM, LET ME WHITEWASH A LITTLE.
I CAN'T DISAPPOINT HER, YOU UNDERSTAND--
NO--NO--I RECKON IT WON'T HARDLY DO, BEN. YOU SEE, AUNT POLLY'S AWFUL PARTICULAR ABOUT THIS FENCE-- RIGHT HERE ON THE STREET YOU KNOW.
OH, COME-- NOW LEMME JUST TRY. I'D LET YOU, IF YOU WAS ME, TOM.
JIM AND SID WERE ASKING TO DO IT, BUT SHE ONLY TRUSTED ME.

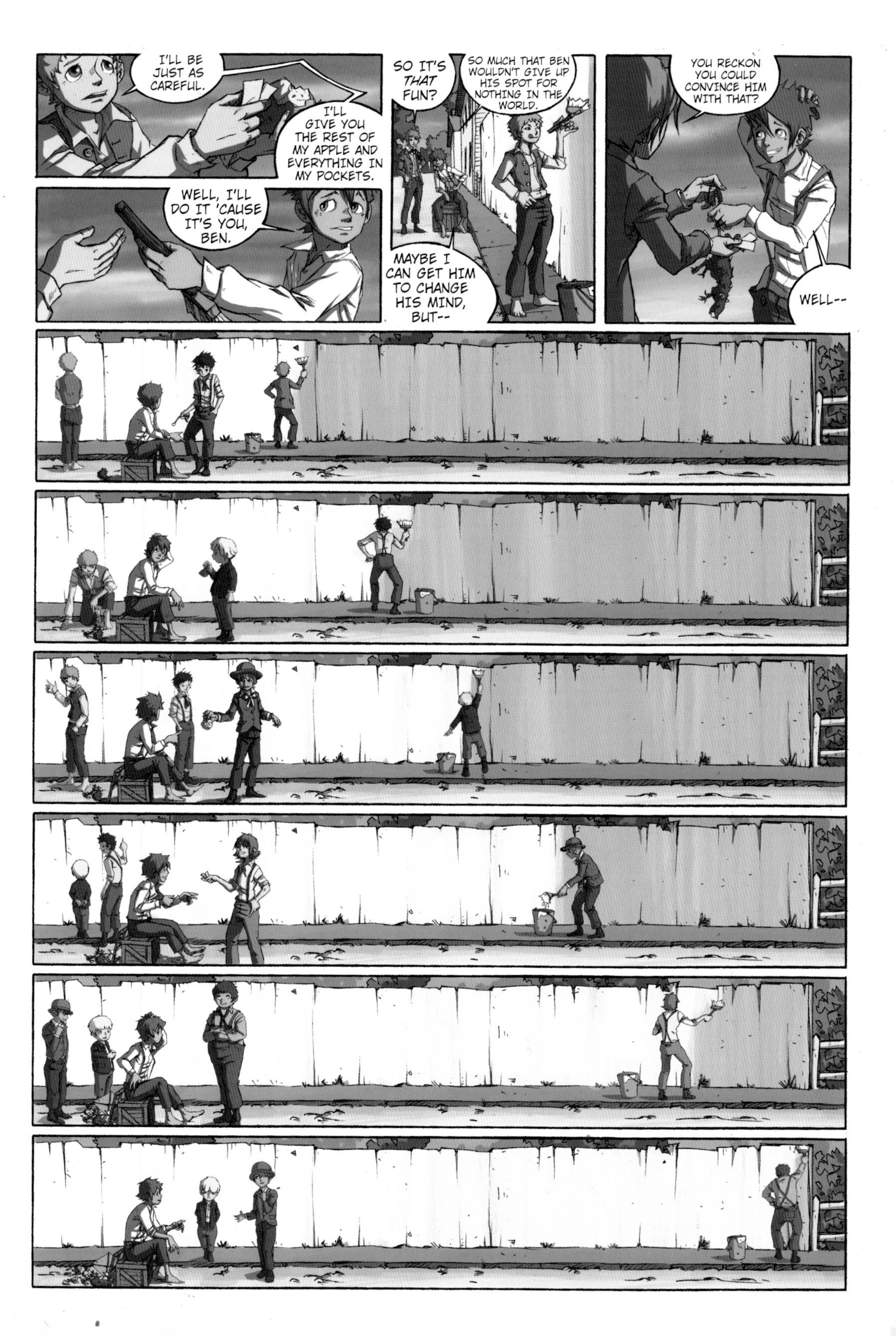
I'LL BE JUST AS CAREFUL.
I'LL GIVE YOU THE REST OF MY APPLE AND EVERYTHING IN MY POCKETS.
WELL, I'LL DO IT 'CAUSE IT'S YOU, BEN.
SO IT'S THAT FUN?
SO MUCH THAT BEN WOULDN'T GIVE UP HIS SPOT FOR NOTHING IN THE WORLD.
MAYBE I CAN GET HIM TO CHANGE HIS MIND, BUT--
YOU RECKON YOU COULD CONVINCE HIM WITH THAT?
WELL--

MAYN'T I GO AND PLAY NOW, AUNT?

WHAT, A'READY? HOW MUCH HAVE YOU DONE?

IT'S ALL DONE.
TOM, DON'T LIE TO ME-I CAN'T BEAR IT.

YOU CAN COME SEE, IF YOU WANT.

WELL, I NEVER! THERE'S NO GETTING ROUND IT, YOU *CAN* WORK WHEN YOU'RE A MIND TO, TOM.

EVEN THOUGH I WAS HOPING SO, I SCARCELY FIGURED I'D BE GIVING YOU THESE TREATS.

THANKS, AUNT POLLY. THEY'LL BE EVEN BETTER 'CAUSE I DID THIS GOOD WORK WITHOUT COVETING 'EM.

WELL, GO 'LONG AND PLAY.
BUT MIND YOU GET BACK IN A WEEK, OR I'LL TAN YOU!
TAP!

NOW I'M AN *ANGEL!*

AUUUUUUUUUUNTT POOOOLLLLYYY!!

TOM GOT ME ALL DIRTY!!

GOOD HEAVENS! HOW CAN A BOY SO NICE AND SMART ALSO BE SO MISCHIEVOUS?

NO WAY. YOU DIDN'T DO THAT--

YOU'D ALREADY GOTTEN SID BACK BY TURNING HIS BED OVER.
HAHAHA, THAT'S WHAT YOU THINK, JOE.

REVENGE IS SOMETHING YOU CHEW ON A LONG TIME.
HAHAHA!

HAHAHA--

WHAT'S WRONG WITH YOU? ARE YOU PARA-LYZED?

TOM?!

IS SHE A FRIEND OF JEFF THATCHER'S?
SHE'S IN HIS YARD.
DO YOU KNOW HER?
NO, 'NEVER SEEN HER--WHY?

I'M IN LOVE.

WHAT ABOUT AMY LAWRENCE?
YOU SAID YOU LOVED HER SOMETHING CRAZY--THAT IT WEREN'T LOVE FOR HER, BUT "ADORATION."

YOU WERE MONTHS WINNING HER. ONLY SEVEN, SHORT DAYS AGO YOU DECLARED YOUR LOVE AND SAID YOU WAS THE HAPPIEST, PROUDEST FELLER IN THE WORLD.
I DON'T EVEN KNOW WHO YOU'RE TALKING ABOUT NOW--

OWW! OUCH!!

--AMEN.

YOU'RE NOT GONNA PRAY BEFORE GOING TO SLEEP?
NO, AND FOR TWO REASONS, SID.
I GOT MY FILL OF SUCH--

--AND I AIN'T FIGURING ON GOING TO BED ANY TIME SOON.

A LIT CANDLE!
I JUST KNEW MY ADORED UNKNOWN WAS WAITING UP FOR ME.

ONCE SHE SEES I KEPT THE FLOWER SHE SENT ME, SHE WON'T BE ABLE TO STOP HERSELF FROM CHASING AFTER ME.

GOSH, SHE DOESN'T HEAR ME.

THERE'S ONLY ONE ANSWER!

CRAK!

STILL, SHE'S OPENING THE WINDOW-

SCAT, YOU CATS!!

TOOOMMMM!!

WHY ARE YOUR CLOTHES ALL WET?
UH,WELL, IS--I FELL ASLEEP STILL DRESSED, RIGHT AFTER PRAYING-- I TRIED SO HARD TO MAKE A GOOD ONE THAT IT COMPLETELY DRAINED ME.

AND I WOKE UP WITH MY CLOTHES ALL SOAKING WITH SWEAT.
HMM, ALL RIGHT FOR THIS TIME.

HAVE YOU FINISHED GOING OVER YOUR LESSONS, BOYS?
LONG SINCE, AUNT.

AND YOU, TOM? YOUR FIVE VERSES FROM THE BIBLE TO RECITE TO THE PASTOR?
I'VE GOT 'EM DOWN LIKE THE TIPS OF MY FINGERS, AUNT POLLY!

I'M LISTEN-ING.
BLESSED ARE THE --A-A--
POOR--
YES; BLESSED ARE THE POOR IN SPIRIT, FOR THEY-THEY-
THEIRS.
FOR THEIRS IS THE KING-DOM OF--

OBVIOUSLY, YOU DON'T HAVE YOUR VERSES ON THE TIPS OF YOUR FIN-GERS.
STUDY A LITTLE MORE, THEN WASH UP AND PUT ON YOUR SUNDAY BEST.

I DON'T LIKE THESE SHOES!!
THEY SQUEEZE MY FEET!

THESE OTHER CLOTHES EITHER--THEY ITCH.

JUST BE HAPPY THE GOOD LORD GAVE YOU THE CHANCE TO HAVE SOME.

NOW, CHILDREN, OUR SUNDAY SCHOOL HAS THE PLEASURE OF WELCOMING SOME ILLUSTRIOUS VISITORS.

SO, I ASK YOU, PLEASE STAND TO HONOR OUR JEFF THATCHER'S FAMILY.

HE IS ACCOMPANIED BY THE VENERABLE COUNTY JUDGE AND HIS FAMILY.

PLEASE, TAKE YOUR SEAT IN OUR PLACE OF HONOR!
TOM SAWYER, WHAT ARE YOU LOOKING AT?

UH--NOTHING-
UH, WELL, THE OLD JUDGE--
HE LOOKS MIGHTY HARSH, DON'T HE?
HMPH--

BILLY, TRADE ME YOUR YALLER TICKET FOR A PIECE OF LICKRISH.
AND A FISHHOOK!

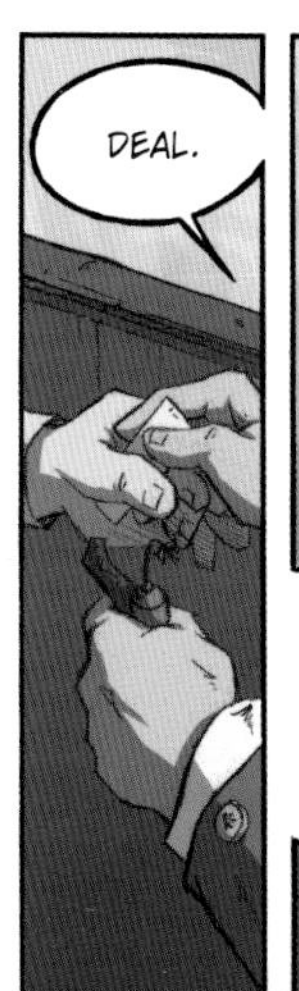
DEAL.

SAY, WILL YA SWAP ME YOUR YALLER TICKETS, JIM?

SAM, 'YOU INTERESTED IN TWO MARBLES FOR A LITTLE PIECE OF YALLER PAPER?

HEY, JACK, YOU'RE MY PAL--
WILL YOU LOAN ME YOUR YALLER TICKETS?

DIRECTLY, I'M GOING TO PRESENT THIS BIBLE ILLUSTRATED BY GUSTAVE DORE TO WHOEVER HAS EARNED THE MOST POINTS.

ANGUS, I THINK YOU HAVE FOUR OF THEM, DON'T YOU?

UH NO, MR. WALTERS, I'VE GOT NINE OF 'EM!
T--
TOM?

YOU LOOKED SURPRISED, SIR.
HERE THEY ARE, YOU CAN COUNT 'EM.

OH,THAT--UH--I DON'T UNDER-STAND HOW--

FINE THEN, INSPECTOR, IS THE TALLY CORRECT?
YES, THAT'S WHAT'S MOST ASTONISHING.

WELL, SO BE IT.
LET'S RENDER JUDGMENT UPON HIM QUICKLY, PLEASE. I'VE OTHER ENGAGEMENTS.

WHAT'S YOUR NAME, MY BOY?
THOMAS SAWYER-- SIR.

THAT'S A GOOD BOY, THOMAS SAWYER.
KNOWLEDGE IS WORTH MORE THAN ANYTHING THERE IS IN THE WORLD.
IT'S WHAT MAKES GREAT MEN AND GOOD MEN.
SOMEDAY, THOMAS, YOU'LL LOOK BACK AND SAY:
"IT'S ALL OWING TO THE PRECIOUS SUNDAY-SCHOOL PRIVILEGES OF MY BOYHOOD."

"IT'S ALL OWING TO THE GOOD SUPERINTENDENT, WHO TAUGHT ME TO LEARN, AND GAVE ME A BEAUTIFUL BIBLE-TO KEEP AND HAVE IT ALL FOR MY OWN."

AND NOW YOU WOULDN'T MIND TELLING ME AND THIS LADY SOME OF THE THINGS YOU'VE LEARNED?

I WOULDN'T KNOW HOW TO CHOOSE--THERE'S TOO MANY, SIR.

I DO UNDERSTAND YOU--IT'S SO RICH.
WON'T YOU TELL US THE NAMES OF THE FIRST TWO DISCIPLES THAT WERE APPOINTED? MY EAR DELIGHTS AT THEIR VERY EVOCATION.

--

AWW, HE'S JUST SHY. YOU'RE INTIMI-DATING HIM, MY DEAR. IT'S CHARMING.

NOW I KNOW YOU'LL TELL ME--
THE NAMES OF THE TWO FIRST TWO DISCIPLES WERE--

DAVID AND GOLIATH?

HEY!

TOM, WHATCHA DOING?

ME, UH-- NOTHING, HUCK, WHY?
'CAUSE THE WEATHER'S GOOD FOR FISHING. WANNA GO TOGETHER?

OH, SORRY, I--I GOTTA GO HOME. YOU KNOW AUNT POLLY.
YEAH, BUT USUALLY, IT DON'T BOTHER YOU TO-

TOO BAD, EH...SOME OTHER TIME--

AND NOW'S IT'S MONDAY--HERE I GOT ANOTHER SCHOOL WEEK UP AND RUN-NING.

TOO BAD I AIN'T SICK--
MY STOMACH HURTS A LITTLE, BUT AUNT POLLY'LL SAY IT'S FROM THE AGONY OF SEEING THE TEACHER AGAIN--

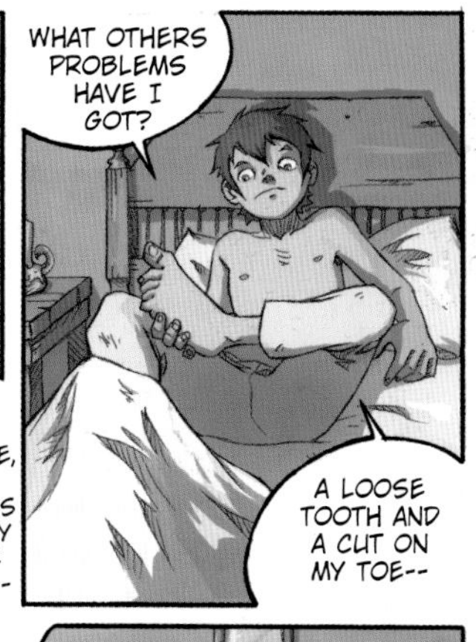
WHAT OTHERS PROBLEMS HAVE I GOT?
A LOOSE TOOTH AND A CUT ON MY TOE--

SID!
SID, HELP!

WHAT'S THE MATTER, TOM?
MY FOOT, I'M A-DYING!!

I'LL GO FETCH AUNT POLLY, SHE'LL SAVE YOU!
I FORGIVE YOU EVERY-THING, SID. EVERYTHING YOU'VE DONE TO ME.

I'LL PICK AT THE SORE SOME, IT'LL MAKE IT MORE REAL.

TOM, MY LITTLE TOM!!

WHAT'S THE MATTER WITH YOU, CHILD?
OH, AUNTIE, MY SORE TOE'S MORTIFIED!

HA HA HA HA!!
WHY, OF COURSE--

STARTED OUT OF MY SLEEP, I PLUMB FORGOT WHAT DAY IT WAS!
IT'S JUST LIKE THE START OF EVERY WEEK!

I WAS SO AFRAID ABOUT MY FOOT, I NEVER MINDED MY TOOTH AT ALL-
YOUR TOOTH, INDEED!

WHAT'S THE MATTER WITH YOUR TOOTH?
ONE OF THEM'S LOOSE, AND IT ACHES PERFECTLY AWFUL.

I'LL CURE YOU!
MARY, GET ME A SILK THREAD AND A CHUNK OF FIRE OUT OF THE KITCHEN!

PLEASE DON'T, AUNTIE!
I DON'T WANT TO STAY HOME FROM SCHOOL. I SWEAR!

MARY, HAND ME EVERYTHING, AND HELP SID HOLD HIS BROTHER!

AAAA!!
AAAA!!

HEY LOOK!
WHAT I CAN DO!

DID YOU SEE, HUCK, 'CAUSE OF MY MISSING A TOOTH, I CAN SPIT SIDE-WAYS!
NICE, AIN'T IT?
YEAH, NOT BAD.

BUT I GOT SOMETHING EVEN BETTER TO SHOW YOU!
WHAT'S THAT YOU GOT?

SPLURT!

WHAT DO YOU SAY ABOUT THAT?
WHOA, A REAL DEAD CAT!
WITH MAGGOTS AND ALL!

WHERE'D YOU GET HIM?
A SWAP.
WHAT DID YOU GIVE?

I GIVE A BLUE TICKET AND A BLADDER THAT I GOT AT THE SLAUGHTER-HOUSE.
WHERE'D YOU GET THE BLUE TICKET?
BOUGHT IT OFF'N BEN ROGERS TWO WEEKS AGO FOR A HOOPSTICK.

SAY--WHAT IS DEAD CATS GOOD FOR, HUCK?
GOOD FOR? CURE WARTS WITH.
NO! IS THAT SO? I KNOW SOMETHING THAT'S BETTER.
I BET YOU DON'T. WHAT IS IT?

WHY, SPUNK WATER!
SPUNK WATER! I WOULDN'T GIVE A DERN FOR SPUNK WATER. D'YOU EVER TRY IT?
NO, I HAIN'T. BUT BOB TANNER DID.
WHO TOLD YOU SO?

WHY, HE TOLD JEFF THATCHER.
AND JEFF TOLD JOHNNY BAKER.
AND JOHNNY TOLD JIM HOLLIS.
AND JIM TOLD BEN ROGERS.
BEN TOLD A BLACK BOY--
AND HE TOLD ME.

WELL, WHAT OF IT? THEY'LL ALL LIE.
LEASTWAYS ALL BUT THE BLACK BOY. I DON'T KNOW HIM. NOW YOU TELL ME HOW BOB TANNER DONE IT.

WHY, HE TOOK AND DIPPED HIS HAND IN A ROTTEN STUMP WHERE THE RAINWATER WAS.
IN THE DAYTIME?
CERTAINLY.

WITH HIS FACE TO THE STUMP?
YES. LEAST I RECKON SO.
DID HE SAY ANY-THING?
MAYBE, I DON'T KNOW.

AHA! TALK ABOUT TRYING TO CURE WARTS WITH SPUNK WATER SUCH A BLAME-FOOL WAY AS THAT! WHY, THAT AIN'T A-GOING TO DO ANY GOOD.

YOU GOT TO GO ALL BY YOURSELF, TO THE MIDDLE OF THE WOODS, WHERE YOU KNOW THERE'S A SPUNK-WATER STUMP--
AND JUST AS IT'S MID-NIGHT YOU BACK UP AGAINST THE STUMP AND JAM YOUR HAND IN AND SAY:

"BARLEY-CORN, BARLEY-CORN, INJUN-MEAL SHORTS, SPUNK WATER, SPUNK WATER, SWALLER THESE WARTS."
AND THEN WALK AWAY QUICK, ELEVEN STEPS, WITH YOUR EYES SHUT, AND THEN TURN AROUND THREE TIMES--
AND WALK HOME WITHOUT SPEAKING TO ANYBODY. BECAUSE IF YOU SPEAK THE CHARM'S BUSTED.

WELL, THAT SOUNDS LIKE A GOOD WAY; BUT THAT AIN'T THE WAY BOB TANNER DONE.
NO, SIR, YOU CAN BET HE DIDN'T, BECUZ HE'S THE WARTIEST BOY IN THIS TOWN; AND HE WOULDN'T HAVE A WART ON HIM IF HE KNOW'D HOW TO WORK SPUNK WATER.

I'VE TOOK OFF THOUSANDS OF WARTS OFF OF MY HANDS THAT WAY. I PLAY WITH FROGS SO MUCH THAT I'VE ALWAYS GOT CONSIDERABLE MANY WARTS.
SOMETIMES I TAKE 'EM OFF WITH A BEAN.

YOU TAKE AND SPLIT THE BEAN--
AND CUT THE WART SO AS TO GET SOME BLOOD--
AND THEN YOU PUT THE BLOOD ON ONE PIECE OF THE BEAN AND BURY IT, 'BOUT MID-NIGHT AT THE CROSSROADS--

IN THE DARK OF THE MOON, AND THEN YOU BURN UP THE REST OF THE BEAN.
YOU SEE, THAT PIECE THAT'S GOT THE BLOOD ON IT WILL KEEP DRAWING, TRY-ING TO FETCH THE OTHER PIECE TO IT-
AND SO THAT HELPS THE BLOOD TO DRAW THE WART, AND PRETTY SOON OFF SHE COMES.

THOUGH WHEN YOU'RE BURYING IT, IF YOU SAY, "DOWN BEAN; OFF WART: COME NO MORE TO BOTHER ME!"-
IT'S BETTER. THAT'S THE WAY JOE HARPER DOES, AND HE'S BEEN NEAR-LY TO COONVILLE AND MOST EVERYWHERES.

AND WHEN IT'S MIDNIGHT A DEVIL WILL COME, OR MAYBE TWO OR THREE, BUT YOU CAN'T SEE 'EM YOU CAN ONLY HEAR SOMETHING LIKE THE WIND, OR MAYBE HEAR 'EM TALK; AND WHEN THEY'RE TAKING THE FELLER AWAY, YOU HEAVE YOUR CAT AFTER 'EM AND SAY, "DEVIL FOLLOW CORPSE, CAT FOLLOW DEVIL, WART FOLLOW CAT, I'M DONE WITH YE!" THAT'LL FETCH ANY WART.

WILL YOU MEOW?
YES--AND YOU MEOW BACK, IF YOU GET A CHANCE.

LAST TIME, YOU KEP' ME A-MEOWING AROUND TILL OLD HAYS WENT TO THROWING ROCKS AT ME AND SAYS "DERN THAT CAT!"

AND SO I HOVE A BRICK THROUGH HIS WINDOW--
BUT DON'T YOU TELL.
I WON'T.

I COULDN'T MEOW THAT NIGHT BECUZ AUNTIE WAS WATCHING ME, BUT I'LL MEOW THIS TIME.

SEE YOU TONIGHT, THEN!

THOMAS SAWYER!!!

LATE AS USUAL, I SEE.
I'M SORRY, I STOPPED TO TALK WITH MY FRIEND HUCKLEBERRY FINN.

THIS IS THE MOST ASTOUNDING CONFESSION I HAVE EVER LISTENED TO.
NO MERE FERULE WILL ANSWER FOR THIS OFFENSE. TAKE OFF YOUR JACKET.

OWW! OUCH!!

NOW, SIR, GO AND SIT WITH THE GIRLS!

AND LET THIS BE A WARNING TO YOU.

SCRITCH!! SCRITCH!!

SCRITCH!! SCRITCH!!

YOU DRAW NICE.
I DO ALL RIGHT--

DRAW ME NOW!
WHAT'S YOUR NAME?

BECKY THATCHER.

DONE--

IT'S EVER SO NICE--I WISH I COULD DRAW.
I'LL LEARN YOU AT NOON. DO YOU GO HOME FOR DINNER?

I'LL STAY IF YOU WILL, THOMAS SAWYER.
THAT'S WHAT THEY CALL ME WHEN SOMETHING'S WRONG.

YOU CALL ME TOM.
WILL YOU?
I PROMISE, TOM.

WHAT DID YOU DRAW THIS TIME, TOM?

I LOVE YOU.

OH, YOU BAD THING!

I DON'T THINK THIS IS WHAT I DICTATED, IS IT?!

WHAT'S MORE, THERE'S A MISTAKE!

HOW MUCH IS 7 TIMES 8, THOMAS SAWYER?

42, TEACHER.
DONG! DONG!
WELL, THAT'S NEW--

SO YOU'VE BEEN SAVED BY THE BELL.

GO AND EAT. I'LL SEE YOU THIS AFTERNOON.

TOM?

AHHH!!

DO YOU LOVE RATS?
NO! I HATE THEM!

WELL, I DO, TOO-- *LIVE* ONES.
BUT I MEAN DEAD ONES, TO SWING ROUND YOUR HEAD WITH A STRING.

YEAH, WELL--

WAS YOU EVER AT A CIRCUS?
OH, YES, I LOVE THAT!

I BEEN TO THE CIRCUS THREE OR FOUR TIMES-- LOTS OF TIMES.
I'M GONNA BE A CLOWN IN A CIRCUS WHEN I GROW UP!

THAT WILL BE REALLY NICE TO MAKE FOLKS LAUGH AND GET SPOTTED UP.
YES, THAT'S SO. AND THEY GET SLATHERS OF MONEY.

SO TELL ME, WHY'D YOU GET ME TO COME BACK TO CLASSROOM DURING THE BREAK?
SAY, BECKY, WAS YOU EVER ENGAGED?
WHAT'S THAT?

WHY, ENGAGED TO BE MARRIED.
NO.
WOULD YOU LIKE TO?
HOW DO YOU DO IT?

IT'S EASY. THE GIRL TELLS THE BOY SHE'LL MARRY ONLY HIM-
AND THEN THEY KISS.

KISS?
DO WE HAVE TO?
WELL YES--THEY ALWAYS DO THAT, COME ON--
YES. DO YOU REMEMBER WHAT I WROTE ON THE SLATE?

I TOLD YOU I LOVE YOU. IT'S YOUR TURN NOW.
IT'S JUST-- I'M A LITTLE AFRAID.

YOU TURN YOUR FACE AWAY, THEN.
I DON'T WANT YOU TO SEE ME.

I-- LOVE-- YOU.

IT'S ALL OVER BUT THE KISS!
NO, TOM, NO--

COME ON, BECKY, JUST A LITTLE KISS.

THERE, NOW WE'LL DO EVERY-THING TOGETHER, JUST LIKE WHEN I WAS WITH AMY.

OH, TOM! THEN I AIN'T THE FIRST YOU'VE EVER BEEN ENGAGED TO!

DON'T CRY, BECKY, YOU'RE THE ONE I LOVE!
THAT'S NOT EVEN TRUE, YOU'RE JUST A LIAR!

BECKY, I-- I DON'T CARE FOR ANYBODY BUT YOU.

HERE, BECKY, IT'S FOR YOU. IT'S MY GREATEST TREASURE.
IT'S YOURS.

SINCE THAT'S HOW IT IS, I'M LEAVING.

YES, I SWEAR TO YOU--IT WAS BIG DEATHWATCH BEETLE!
IF YOU HEAR SUCH AS THOSE, IT MEANS SOMEBODY'S GONNA DIE SOON!
DON'T TELL ME YOU BELIEVE SUCH ROT.
OF COURSE NOT, WHAT DO YOU TAKE ME FOR?

DO YOU BELIEVE THE DEAD PEOPLE LIKE IT FOR US TO BE HERE?
I WISHT I KNOWED. IT'S AWFUL SOLEMN LIKE, *AIN'T* IT?

WELL, NOW WE HAVE TO VISIT HOSS WILLIAM'S GRAVE.
'CAREFUL ABOUT WHAT YOU SAY!

WHY'S THAT? EVERYBODY CALLS HIM HOSS!
'CAN'T BE TOO PARTICULAR HOW YOU TALK 'BOUT THESE YER DEAD PEOPLE.

LET'S GET HERE. IT'LL BE PERFECT.
WE'RE DOOMED!

WHAT ARE YOU TALKING ABOUT?
IT'S DEVIL-FIRE DOWN YONDER!

NO, ONE OF 'EM'S OLD MUFF POTTER'S VOICE.
AND IT'S NOT A LIGHT.
DRUNK, THE SAME AS USUAL, LIKELY--BLAMED OLD RIP!

BAD NEWS, ONE'S OF 'EM'S INJUN JOE.

HE'S ALWAY MIXED UP IN BAD DEALINGS!
LET'S HIDE IN HERE!

PLEASE, GENTLEMEN. LET'S NOT WASTE TIME.

THE CUSSED THING'S READY, SAWBONES.
AND YOU'LL JUST OUT WITH ANOTHER FIVE, OR HERE SHE STAYS.
THAT'S THE TALK!

WHAT DOES THIS MEAN?
I ALREADY PAID YOU IN ADVANCE!
THE DEBT BETWEEN THE TWO OF US IS A LOT BIGGER THAN THAT, DOC!

HOW'S THAT?
ONE DAY WHEN I WAS A YOUNGSTER, I CAME TO BEG FOR A BIT OF BREAD AT YOUR PRETTY HOUSE. YOU RAN ME OFF--AND YOUR FATHER HAD ME JAILED FOR A VAGRANT.

SO I SAY IT'S TIME TO SETTLE OUR SCORE--
BRIGAND!

DON'T YOU HIT MY PARD!
IF YOU THINK I'M GOING TO LET MYSELF BE ABUSED--

I WAS THE BOXING CHAMPION AT THE UNIVERSITY!

HMMPF!

AND I'VE STILL GOT A FEW LICKS IN ME!

HEY, COME ON, WE CAN'T STAY HERE.

THAT SCORE IS SETTLED-- DAMN YOU.

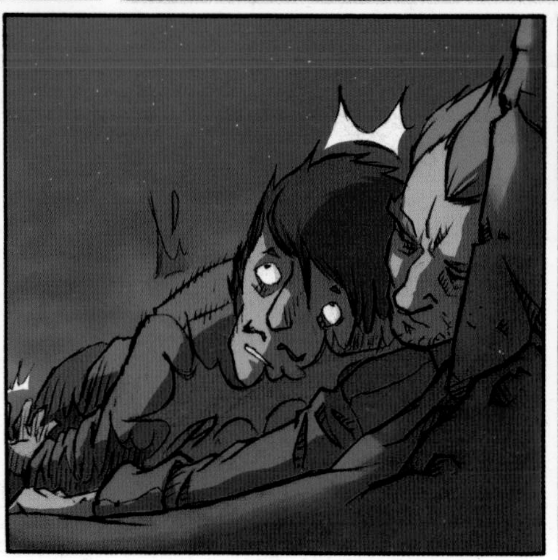

LORD, HOW IS THIS, JOE?
IT'S A DIRTY BUSINESS. WHAT DID YOU DO IT FOR?

ME?!
BUT I-I NEVER DONE IT!
THAT KIND OF TALK WON'T WASH. YOU STILL HAVE THE KNIFE IN YOUR HAND.

IT'S AWFUL. BUT I DIDN'T THINK I WAS DRUNK TONIGHT. HOW DID I DO THAT?
YOU TWO WAS SCUFFLING, AND AFTER HE FETCHED YOU ONE ON THE CHIN, YOU STABBED HIM IN THE HEART.

OH, I DIDN'T KNOW WHAT I WAS A-DOING. I'VE NEVER KILLED A MAN--
I AIN'T NO MURDERER!
THERE'S ALWAYS A FIRST TIME, YOU KNOW.

IT'S NOT MY FAULT. IT WAS THE WHISKY!
YOU'VE ALWAYS BEEN A GOOD FRIEND. I WON'T TELL.
WE'LL ACT LIKE WE DON'T KNOW EACH OTHER.

THANKS, JOE, YOU'RE AN ANGEL.

I KNOW, I KNOW.
NOW, GET MOVING!

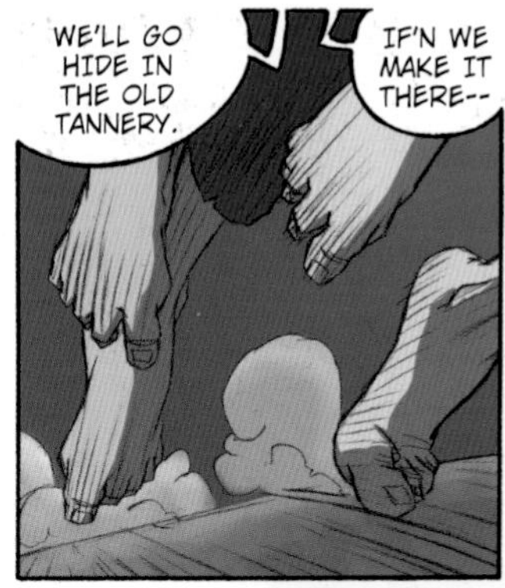
WE'LL GO HIDE IN THE OLD TANNERY.
IF'N WE MAKE IT THERE--

COME ON, HUCK, WE'RE ALMOST THERE!

WHAT DO YOU RECKON'LL COME OF THIS?
IF DR. ROBINSON DIES, I RECKON HANGING'LL COME OF IT.

ANYHOW, I AIN'T ONE TO BE BLABBING TO THE SHERIFF--
YOU'RE RIGHT. S'POSE SOME HAPPENED AND INJUN JOE *DIDN'T* HANG? WHY, HE'D KILL US!

IT AIN'T GONNA BE EASY TO KEEP TWO MURDERS TO OURSELVES--
WE CAN'T FORGET ABOUT MUFF POTTER!

HE WAS JUST KNOCKED OUT--HE HAD HIS LIQUOR IN HIM.
IT'S JUST LIKE WITH MY PAP.

YOU SURE YOU CAN KEEP MUM?
LET'S SWEAR TO ONE ANOTHER TO KEEP MUM TILL OUR DYING DAY!

OH, NO, THAT'S GOOD ENOUGH FOR LITTLE RUBBISHY COMMON THINGS--ESPECIALLY WITH GALS.
WE GOT TO MAKE A BLOOD OATH.
AN OATH?
YOU'RE RIGHT. THAT'S WHAT WE GOT TO DO.

HUCK FINN AND TOM SAWYER SWEARS THEY WILL KEEP MUM ABOUT THIS AND THEY WISH THEY MAY DROP DOWN DEAD IN THEIR TRACKS IF THEY EVER TELL AND ROT.
NOW WE JUST GOT TO SIGN IN BLOOD.

WHO'D HAVE KNOWN THIS NEEDLE FOR MY COLLAR WOULD EVER BE SO IMPORTANT-

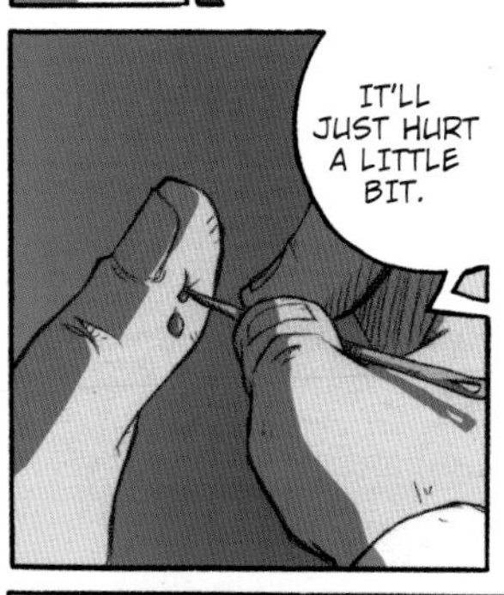
IT'LL JUST HURT A LITTLE BIT.

TWO STRAIGHT STICKS GOING FROM THE SKY TO THE GROUND AND A LITTLE BAR CONNECTING 'EM IN THE MIDDLE.

THAT'S NOT SOME PIDDLING OATH!

OHHHHH!!

OH, WHAT'S THAT HOWLING?!
IT'S LIKE IT CAME FROM THE OTHER SIDE OF THE WALL.
MAYBE IT'S A STRAY DOG?!
STRANGE DOG!! SOUNDS LIKE--LIKE HOGS GRUNTING.

GIMME A BOOST, I'LL LOOK OUT THROUGH THE WINDOW.
ALL RIGHT!

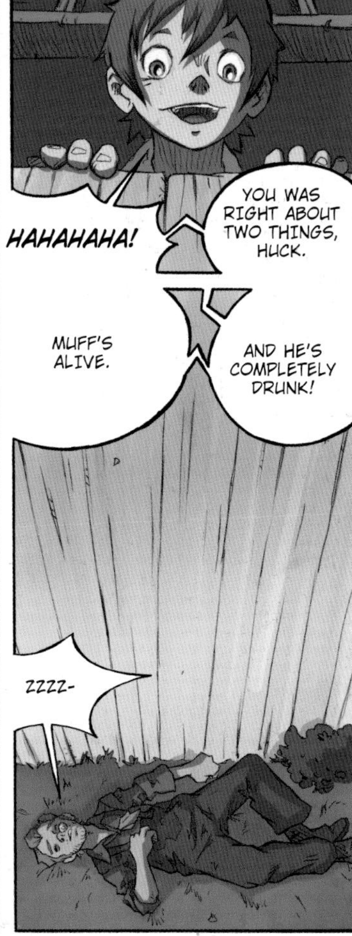
HAHAHAHA!
YOU WAS RIGHT ABOUT TWO THINGS, HUCK.
MUFF'S ALIVE.
AND HE'S COMPLETELY DRUNK!
ZZZZ-

LINE UP IN TWO FILES, AND COME IN QUIETLY.

IS THAT SEAT BESIDE YOU FREE, AMY?
OF COURSE, BECKY--

DIING!
DIING!
DIING!

DIING!
DIIING!
IT'S TIME, YOU CAN GO HOME.

I'LL GIVE YOU A TEST ON THE LESSON TOMORROW DURING FIRST PERIOD.

'THINGS NOT GOING WELL, TOM?

YESSIR, OF COURSE, WHY WOULDN'T THEY BE?
IN ALL THE TIME I'VE HAD YOU AS MY PUPIL, IT'S THE FIRST TIME YOU'VE EVER BEEN THE LAST TO LEAVE.

EXCEPTING THE TIME YOU FELL ASLEEP, OF COURSE.

BECKY...

MY LITTLE FIANCÉE, WAIT UP!

WHY, OF COURSE, TOM.
JUST TELL US WHICH ONE YOU WANTED TO TALK WITH!

TEEHEEHEE HEEHEE!!

TEEHEEHEE HEEHEE!!

TEEHEEHEE HEEHEE!!

HE'S BEEN KNIFED!
THEY FOUND THE GORY BLADE RIGHT BESIDE THE TWO CORPSES!
IT WAS MUFF POTTER'S KNIFE!

A FISHERMAN SAW HIM WARSHING HISSELF IN THE RIVER ABOUT TWO O'CLOCK IN THE MORNING.
AND YOU WOULDN'T SAY IT WAS HABIT FOR WASHING THAT GOT HIM UP AT NIGHT...
?!

I SWEAR I DIDN'T SEE YOU STAB THE DOC, JOE!

OH, NO, IT'S JUST ME; HUCK.
WHEWWW. YOU SCARED ME.
I KNOW WHAT YOU MEAN. I'M AS HIGH STRUNG AS YOU.

ALL THE MORE SO SINCE THE MURDERER AIN'T THAT FAR OFF.

HE'S REALLY GOT A LOT OF GALL DARING TO COME HERE.

I SEE HIM!!
AT THE EDGE OF THE FOREST!!
MUFF POTTER!

BRING'M TO ME RIGHT NOW!

I DIDN'T DO IT FRIENDS! 'PON MY WORD AND HONOR I NEVER DONE IT.

WHO'S ACCUSED YOU?

BUT, I...
HE DIDN'T...
NO, THEN...

INJUN JOE, YOU PROMISED ME YOU'D NEVER SAY A THING!

IS THAT YOUR KNIFE?
YES, YES. I'M SORRY, BUT I'M FEEL-ING KINDA WEAK.

TELL 'EM, JOE, TELL 'EM-- IT AIN'T ANY USE ANY MORE.
IF YOU WANT, POOR OLD MUFF.

LET ME TELL THE WHOLE TRUTH. THAT'LL LET YOU PLEAD GUILTY AND HAVE ATTENUATING CIRCUMSTANCES.

HE'S ONE STONYHEARTED LIAR!
AND WHAT'S MORE, EVERYBODY BELIEVES 'M!
THEY'RE BEWITCHED.
HE'S A REAL DEMON!
'BET HE'S SOLD HIS SOUL TO THE DEVIL!
IF WE WAS TO SAY WHAT WE SAW TO THE SHERIFF, THE DEVIL'D TELL JOE WHERE TO FIND US, AND...
IF WE WATCHED HIM AT NIGHTS, I RECKON WE'D END UP SEEING HIS DREAD MASTER.
IT'D BE MIGHTY TERRIFYING!
THERE'S ONE THING I DON'T UNDERSTAND, MUFF POTTER:
WHY DIDN'T YOU LEAVE? WHAT DID YOU WANT TO COME HERE FOR?
I WANTED TO RUN AWAY, BUT I COULDN'T HELP IT.
I COULDN'T HELP IT.
I KNOW WHAT HE MEANS. I ENDED UP HERE WITHOUT MEANING TO.
ME, TOO.
IT'S TIME WE GOT GOING.

WELL NOW, TOM, SO YOU'RE NOT EATING?
I'M NOT VERY HUNGRY, AUNTIE.
IT MUST BE GROWIN' PAINS. YOU'D BETTER GET ON TO BED.
THANK YOU, AUNT POLLY. GOOD NIGHT.
NO!
>HRNNN<
IT'S BLOOD.
I DON'T WANNA DIE!!!

NO, I'M MUFF POTTER. YOU'LL BE THE DOCTOR.

HEY, TOM, ARE YOU GONNA PLAY MURDER IN THE CEMETERY WITH US?
NOT ME.
PLEASE COME ON. WE NEED SOMEBODY TO PLAY INJUN JOE.

WHAT'S WRONG WITH HIM?
HE USUALLY LIKES PLAYING THE BAD GUYS.

TOM'S PITCHING AROUND AND TALKING IN HIS SLEEP SO MUCH THAT HE KEEPS ME AWAKE HALF THE TIME.
WHAT ARE YOU TALKING ABOUT, SID?
FOR TWO NIGHTS, HE'S BEEN BEL-LOWING "IT'S BLOOD!"
OR "LET ME LIVE!!!"
WHAT HAVE YOU GOT ON YOUR MIND, TOM?

NOTHING, AUNTIE, I SWEAR. JUST A FEW NIGHTMARES, NOTHING MORE.

OH, BE CAREFUL!
I DIDN'T MEAN TO.
AND YOU EVEN SAID, "DON'T TORMENT ME SO --I'LL TELL!"

THAT AIN'T TRUE!
WHATEVER YOU SAY.

IT'S THAT DREADFUL MURDER THAT'S BOTHERING ALL OF US.
THAT'S RIGHT. I'VE HAD SOME NIGHTMARES ABOUT IT MYSELF.

MY POOR, LITTLE TOM, YOU'RE A SENSITIVE FELLER AFTER ALL.
IN MY DREAM, IT WAS THE INDIAN COMING TO STRANGLE ME.

IT'S TIME TO GET GOING, MY DEARS, OR YOU'LL BE LATE FOR SCHOOL.

NOW WHERE'S MY SANDWICH?

>PSSTTT,< MUFF.

'S' THAT YOU AGAIN, BOY? IT'S NICE KNOWING SOME-ONE OUT YON-DER'S THINKING ABOUT ME.

YOU'RE SPOILING ME AGAIN. WHY ARE YOU TREAT-ING ME SO SPECIAL?
OH, IT AIN'T HARDLY NOTHING. I'LL BE BACK TOMORROW.

I'LL BE HERE.
I AIN'T GOT A CHOICE IN ANY CASE.

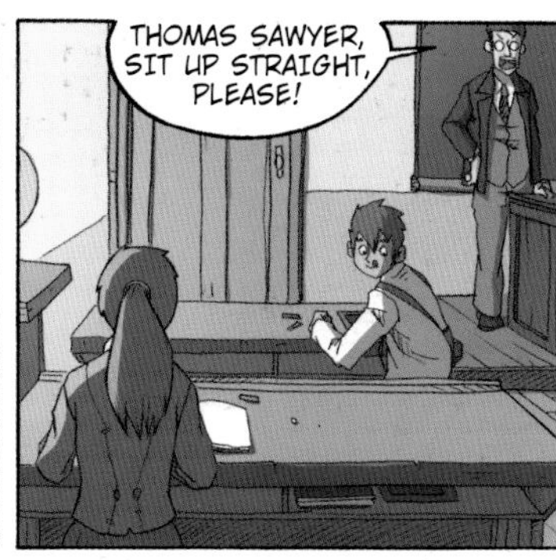
THOMAS SAWYER, SIT UP STRAIGHT, PLEASE!

JOE, DID YOU SEE BECKY THATCHER'S NOT HERE TODAY!
YEAH. BOTH OF YOU WERE ABSENT YESTERDAY.

DON'T FORGET TO STUDY. I'LL BE QUIZZING YOU TOMORROW!
DON'T FORGET, EH, JOE?
YOU CAN COUNT ON ME.

WOULD YOU FIND OUT ABOUT AMY FOR ME, 'CAUSE I, WELL...
YOU KNOW.
DON'T FRET IT. I'LL FIND OUT.

BECKY'S ILL. IT MAY BE SERIOUS. THEY DON'T REALLY KNOW.
ILL.
SERIOUS.

I'LL COME BY AND SEE HER AGAIN TOMORROW. TILL THEN, THREE THINGS: REST, REST, AND REST.
THANK YOU, DOCTOR.

WELL, MY BOY, YOU DON'T LOOK ALL THAT HEARTY AT THE MOMENT.

DON'T YOU WORRY YOURSELF. YOUR AUNT POLLY'S GONNA TAKE CARE OF YOU RIGHT AWAY!

I'M NOT SOME NOVICE ABOUT GENTLE TREATMENTS!

WE HAVE TO BELIEVE OUR EYES. HE'S NOT GETTING ANY BETTER!
TIME TO GET SERIOUS.

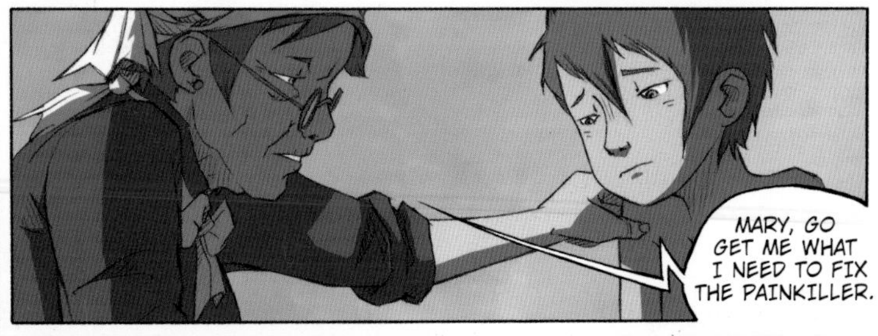
MARY, GO GET ME WHAT I NEED TO FIX THE PAINKILLER.

THE PAINKILLER!! ARE YOU SURE?

THE SITUATION DEMANDS IT!

DOES THAT SMELL STRONG ENOUGH, AUNT POLLY?
NO, LET'S ADD A BIT OF BRUSSELS SPROUT ROOTS.
AND SOME PORK RIND.

YUCK, I DON'T KNOW WHETHER IF I WANT YOU TO RUB THAT STUFF ON ME.

PERFECT!!

TOM, MY DEAR, YOUR SYRUP IS READY.
WHAT?! SO THAT'S FOR DRINK-ING?!!

COME ON, OPEN UP!

ALL RIGHT, IS IT GOOD?

IT'S DELICIOUS.

BLAHHHHHHHHH!
?

FOR PERKING UP...
...THAT'LL DO THE JOB!
MRROWW!!

IT'S NOT TRUE?!!

BE-E-CKY IS BACK, HURRAH!
BE-E-CKY IS BACK, WOOHOO!

BECKY IS WELLL!!

HEY, MY CAP!!!!

MF! SOME PEOPLE THINK THEY'RE SO SMART--ALWAYS SHOWING OFF!
ANNOYING. COME ON, BECKY.

BECKY...

IT'S A SIGN. A SCHOOLBOY'S LIFE AIN'T FOR ME!
FROM NOW ON, I'M BECOMING AN OUTLAW!

OR BETTER YET...
...A PIRATE CAPTAIN!!!
AND I'LL BE YOUR SECOND-IN-COM-MAND, ALL RIGHT?!!

BOARD
THEIR SHIP!!

FREE BECKY THATCHER, YOU BLACK-HEARTED ENGLISHMAN!

DON'T COUNT ON IT!!

THAT'S THE FIRST TIME YOU'VE ASKED ME TO NOT COUNT!
AND YOU'RE GONNA REGRET IT!

TAKE THAT, JEFF THATCHER!
I'VE GOT JUST AS MUCH FOR YOU, JOHNNY MILLER!

WE HAVE PREVAILED, MY FRIENDS!
THE GALLEON'S TREASURE IS YOURS!

WELL?!

HOW DOES IT FEEL TO BE WEARING THE OTHER SHOES?

TOM...

DON'T LOWER YOURSELF TO HIS LEVEL, MY HERO, I BEG YOU. THE SHAME OF DEFEAT WILL SUFFICE FOR HIM.

I WILL BE MAG-NANIMOUS FOR YOUR SAKE.
UH, MAGMANA-MOUS.
UMM, ALL RIGHT, I'LL STOP FOR NOW.

HOW KIND YOU ARE. AND ISN'T THE WEATHER BETTER FOR TAKING A WALK THAN A TORTURE SESSION?

YOU'RE RIGHT, MY DARLING. SUCH ROMANTIC MOMENTS AS THESE ARE TOO RARE IN A PIRATE'S LIFE.
YET, BENEATH YOUR IRON MUSCLES, I'M CERTAIN THERE BEATS A TENDER HEART.

BECKY ...
TOM...

OH, YEAH, SO YOU'RE KISSING SIDES OF BACON NOW?

YOU'D DO BETTER TO HELP US...

"...GATHER SOME WOOD...

"...SET UP THE TENT...

"...START A FIRE...

"...REPAIR THE RAFT THAT SANK...

"... FISH SOME WHOPPERS...

...FIX OUR MEAL..."

A PIRATE'S LIFE SURE IS A GOOD ONE.

STILL, I FIGURED IT'D BE LESS TIRING.

YES, AUNT POLLY, I'M GETTING UP. I'LL BE ON TIME FOR SCHOOL.

WHAT A NIGHTMARE.
TODAY, THERE'S NO MORE BOOKS, NO MORE LESSONS, NO MORE BELL, AND NOT EVEN A TOM!!

I'M THE BLACK AVENGER OF THE SPANISH MAIN!!
AND I'M FRREEEEE!!!

I CAN SPEND MY TIME WATCHING THE LIVES OF BUGS WITHOUT EVEN FEELING GUILTY.

YOU DIDN'T LOOK TOO GUILTY WHEN WE PLAYED HOOKY TOGETHER.

THAT'S RIGHT, I RECKON.

BUT BEING A PIRATE LETS YOU GET THROUGH THE DAY WITHOUT GETTING ANY LICKS.

COME ON LAZY-BONES, IT'S TIME FOR A BATH!

I'M STARTING TO GET COLD.
I'M HUNGRY AS A HORSE!

WE COULD FISH OVER YONDER!
LET'S GO!
I'LL TEND TO THE FIRE.

THAT WAS GOOD.
DEE-LI-SHUS!
LET'S GO EXPLORING!

SO YOU DARE TO MEASURE YOURSELF AGAINST THE TERROR OF THE SEAS?
I FEAR NO MAN, NOT HUCK FINN THE RED-HANDED.
THE BLACK AVENGER WILL BATTLE THE WINNER.

POW!
CRACK!
BANG!

HMM, THIS WATER'S SO PURE.
A MASSACRE

YEAH, THAT'S WHAT WATER TASTES LIKE FROM THE WELL NEAR THE FARM.

BOOOM!
HEY, A STORM'S A-BREWING ON THE OTHER SIDE OF THE RIVER.
IF WE WAS SMART, WE'D GO FIND SOME COVER.

BUT THAT REALLY AIN'T US!!!

BOOOOM!

BOOOOMMMM!

TAIN'T THUNDER AFTER ALL.
BOOOOOOOM!

'FUNNY WAY OF FISHING.
THEY LOOKING FOR SOMEBODY WHO'S DROWNDED. THEY DONE THAT LAST SUMMER, WHEN BILL TURNER GOT DROWNDED.

OH, YEAH, THE BALLS MAKE THE MUCK AND BODIES STUCK IN IT RISE TO THE TOP.
I WISH I WAS OVER THERE, NOW. I'D GIVE HEAPS TO KNOW WHO IT IS.

I KNOW WHO'S DROWND-ED, BOYS.

THEN WHY WON'T YOU TELL US?
I JUST DID.
SO I'LL SAY IT AGAIN: BOYS. ME..

HIM, YOU...
...Y'ALL.

IT'S US!

ONCE I FIGURED OUT IT WAS US THEY WERE LOOKING FOR IN THE WATER, I FELT LIKE A HERO IN AN INSTANT!

WE WERE MISSED; WE WERE MOURNED! TOO CLEVER!

MAYBE FOLKS WERE EVEN REGRETTING BEING UNKIND TO US! MAYBE EVEN THE TEACHER WAS BEING REMORSEFUL!!

AND THEN AS THE EXCITEMENT WORE OFF, I STARTED TO HAVE SOME MISGIVINGS, TOO.

I STARTED THINKING ABOUT AUNT POLLY, MARY AND EVEN SID, WHO ALL MUST BE MIGHTY SAD THINKING ME DEAD. IT WAS KEEPING ME FROM SLEEPING. I HAD TO FIND OUT.

SINCE YOU WERE GIVING EACH OTHER A HARD TIME ABOUT IT, I TIPTOED OFF.

ONCE I WAS IN THE MISSISSIPPI, I CLIMBED INTO A SKIFF ATTACHED BEHIND THE STEAMBOAT.

WE'D ALREADY DONE IT PLENTY OF TIMES, HUCK, TO TRAVEL FOR FREE!

I SLIPPED OVERBOARD BEFORE ARRIVING, SO AS TO NOT GET SPOTTED BY ANY STRAGGLERS GETTING OFF THE BOAT.

AND I TOOK THE LIT-TLE-USED ALLEYS TO REACH THE HOUSE.

THERE SAT AUNT POLLY, SID, MARY, AND JOE HARPER'S MOTHER.

BUT I COULDN'T HEAR ANYTHING, SO I CREPT INSIDE WITHOUT MAKING A NOISE.

QUAKING EVERY TIME IT CREAKED, I STARTED SWEATING.

HE WAS A GOOD BOY, MY JOE!
YES, JUST LIKE MY TOM, ALWAYS FULL OF DEVILMENT AND MISCHIEF, BUT HE WARN'T BAD.
I COULD FINALLY MAKE OUT WHAT THEY WERE SAYING.

AND THE LAST WORDS I EVER HEARD HIM SAY WAS TO REPROACH--

NOT A WORD AGAINST TOM!
I KNOW JUST HOW YOU FEEL.

I HOPE TOM'S BETTER OFF WHERE HE IS.
BUT IF HE'S BEEN BETTER IN SOME WAYS--

OH, SID! DON'T SAY THAT!

ONLY LAST SATURDAY MY JOE BUSTED A FIRECRACK-ER RIGHT UNDER MY NOSE.

I KNOCKED HIM SPRAWLING, BUT NOW I'D HUG HIM.
I'M SO MAD WITH MYSELF.
I'M THE SAME.
I FEEL GUILTY.

IT'S MY FAULT IF HE DROWNED AFTER FALLING OFF THAT RAFT.

OH, ME TOO! I COULDN'T SEE I WAS BEING TOO HARSH WITH HIM. HE WAS UNHAPPY.

OH! MRS. HARPER, HOW MANY MORE TRIALS MUST WE STILL ENDURE!

I REFUSE TO CONTEMPLATE IT. I CANNOT BRING MYSELF TO HAVE THE FUNERAL SERVICE ON SUNDAY.

THERE'S STILL SOME HOPE. OUR TOM WAS A GOOD SWIMMER, AND CLEVER TOO.
I'M LOSING HOPE. THE SEARCH PARTIES HAVEN'T TURNED UP A THING.

IT'S LATE. I'M GOING TO LET YOU GET SOME REST.
WE'RE GOING TO NEED OUR STRENGTH AND WE HAVE HARDLY ANY AT ALL.

'SEE YOU TOMORROW, MRS. HARPER.

SINCE I COULDN'T LEAVE, I HAD TO WAIT FOR EVERYONE TO GO TO BED.

AUNT POLLY'S GRIEF DIDN'T PASS.

I SWEAR TO YOU THAT IT STARTED AFFECTIN' ME.

EVEN PIRATES HAVE GOT A HEART.

BUT THEN SOMETHING OCCURRED TO ME...

I BEG YOUR FORGIVE-NESS, AUNTIE, FOR ALL THE PAIN I'M CAUSING YOU.

THAT WAY YOU'LL KNOW I'M THINKING ABOUT YOU.

LUCKILY, I CAUGHT MYSELF AT THE LAST MINUTE!

WELL, ALMOST.

I DON'T HAVE ANY STORIES ABOUT MY RETURN.

'SORRY FOR THINKING YOU WERE A COWARDLY DESERTER, TOM.

I KNEW YOU WERE LOYAL, I KNEW YOU WERE TOO PROUD FOR THAT AND WOULD COME BACK.

LET'S NOT MENTION IT ANY MORE, BOYS.
SO, ARE WE HEADING BACK?
NO, NEVER!!

NO, WE'RE PIRATES, THERE'S NO WAY WE'RE CHICKENING OUT!
YEAH, I WAS JUST WANTING TO TEST YOU, BUT YOU DIDN'T FALL FOR IT. GOOD JOB!!

IT'S A DEAL!

PIRATES FOR LIFE, PIRATES TO THE DEATH...

CRAACK
BROOOM!
I WANNA GO HOME AND SEE MY MAMA!
JUST WAIT, IT'LL PASS. JUST THINK OF ALL THE GOOD FISHING AND SWIMMING!
I DON'T CARE ABOUT ALL THAT!
OH, THE CRYBABY WANTS TO SEE HIS MAMA!
YES, AND IF YOU HAD ONE, YOU'D DO LIKE ME.
GO 'LONG HOME. WE'LL STAY, WON'T WE, HUCK?
WELL, YOU GOTTA ADMIT THIS DON'T LOOK LIKE IT'S BLOWING OVER.
HUCK AND ME AIN'T CRYBABIES!
HA HA HA!
I STILL THINK WE'D DO BETTER TO LEAVE THIS CAMP BEFORE IT GETS FLOODED.
AND US WITH IT.
WELL, GO 'LONG, IF YOU WANT TO! I DON'T NEED YOU.
GOOD RIDDANCE!!
CRAAK!
HEY, BOYS!
WAIT! WAIT!
I HAVE A GREAT PLAN!!

THEY'VE CALLED OFF THE SEARCH.
THERE'S NO MORE HOPE.
HOW TRAGIC.
POOR CHILDREN.
AIN'T IT JUST AWFUL?
THE MISSISSIPPI WILL RETURN THE BODIES ONE DAY.

SHHHH
SHHHH
THERE'S THE FAMILY.

BROTHERS AND SISTERS IN CHRIST. I AM THE RESURRECTION AND THE LIFE.

WELL, THEY ALL LOOK MIGHTY SAD.
THESE WORDS WERE SPOKEN TO MARTHA, THE SISTER OF LAZARUS, AT THE MOMENT WHEN SHE WAS WEEPING FOR HER DEAD BROTHER.
THE LORD HAS CALLED HOME TOM, A KIND RASCAL WITH A BIG HEART...
...WHO SOMETIMES PILFERED THINGS TO GENEROUSLY NOURISH HIS FRIEND HUCK.

AND LITTLE JOE, WHO LOVED HIS MOTHER SO AND WHO DID KIND DEEDS FOR HIS DEAR ONES.
EVEN LITTLE HUCK WAS A CREATURE OF A GOD WHO LOVED HIM.

IN THE FACE OF THIS MISFORTUNE THAT HAS BEFALLEN OUR COMMUNITY, WE MUST REAFFIRM OUR TOGETHERNESS, SO THAT FRIENDSHIP WILL REKINDLE OUR BEREFT HEARTS.

LET'S SING ALL TOGETHER!
AMAZING GRACE! HOW SWEET THE SOUND THAT SAVED A WRETCH LIKE ME! I ONCE WAS LOST, BUT NOW AM FOUND; WAS BLIND, BUT NOW I SEE.

UHHH?!!

UHHH?!!!

I AM SO HAPPY MY TOM'S BEEN RETURNED TO ME!
I'M SO HAPPY. IT'S THE BEST DAY OF MY LIFE!
TOOOOOM'S BACK!

MY JOE, MY LITTLE BOY. I WAS SO GRIEVED. I LOVE YOU SO MUCH.

AUNT POLLY, IT AIN'T FAIR. SOMEBODY'S GOT TO BE GLAD TO SEE HUCK.

YOU'RE RIGHT, MY LITTLE TOM.
I'M SO HAPPY TO SEE YOU AGAIN, TOO, HUCK. YOU MUSTN'T LEAVE US EVER AGAIN!

OH, THE GREAT SOUL THAT REMEMBERS HIS LITTLE FRIEND. PRAISE BE TO GOD!

I TOLD YOU AHEAD OF TIME IT'D END UP PERFECT!

LET'S GO, TOM, WE'RE GOING TO TAKE GOOD CARE OF YOU.

HA HA, THERE'S NO MORE CALL FOR SPANKINGS. YOU'RE A GOOD BOY NOW. I WAS THINKING MORE ON A NICE MEAL.
AS THOUGH WE WANTED TO DO ANYTHING TO HIM.
WE'RE WAY TOO HAPPY HE'S COME HOME!

NO, AUNT POLLY! NO LICKS WITH YOUR SLIPPERS!

WE'RE GONNA MAKE YOU SOME PANCAKES!!
SID, GO FETCH SOME NICE, FRESH WATER FOR TOM.

ISN'T THAT JUST WHAT YOU LIKE WITH SOME JELLY?
STILL, YOU COULD HAVE LET US KNOW YOU WERE ALL RIGHT.

WE MUSTN'T BE ANGRY WITH HIM. HE'S ALWAYS IN SUCH A RUSH THAT HE NEVER THINKS OF ANYTHING.
I'M SORRY, BUT I DREAMED ABOUT YOU, ANYWAY. THAT'S SOMETHING, AIN'T IT?

A NIGHTMARE OR...
NOT AT ALL! SID AND MARY WERE ON THE WOODBOX, MRS. HARPER ON THE BED, AND YOU WERE IN YOUR CHAIR. THE CANDLE WAS GOING OUT. YOU SAID A DRAFT WAS COMING THROUGH THE OPEN DOOR.

THAT'S JUST HOW IT HAPPENED.
AMAZING! AND?
SID SAID SOMETHING KIND OF BAD ABOUT ME, AND YOU SHUT HIM UP SHARP. AND MRS. HARPER TALKED ABOUT JOE SCARING HER WITH A FIRECRACKER, AND YOU TOLD ABOUT PETER AND THE PAINKILLER.

SINCE I COULD SEE HOW SAD YOU WERE, I TOOK AND WROTE ON A PIECE OF SYCAMORE BARK, "WE AIN'T DEAD," AND PUT IT NEAR YOUR BED AFTER HAVING KISSED YOU.
'A LITTLE SILLY, AIN'T IT?

NOT AT ALL, IT'S VERY TOUCHING. I JUST FORGIVE YOU EVERYTHING FOR THAT!
GIVE ME A HUG, MY BOY.

IT'S GREAT BEING HEROES AFTER HAVING BEEN PIRATES.
YEAH, EVERYBODY ADMIRES US. THEY DREAM OF BEING US.

HEY, THERE'S THE FLOCK.
WITH THAT FAKE, LITTLE BECKY THATCHER LEADING THE WAY.

BUT I THOUGHT SHE WAS YOUR GIRL-FRIEND?
THAT WAS BEFORE. NOW I REALLY DON'T CARE. HERE SHE COMES. I'LL SEE YOU.

HEY, FELLOWS, ARE YOU KEEN ON A PIRATE STORY?

SAY, JOE, DID TOM SAY ANY-THING ABOUT ME TO YOU?
AH UH, NO, UM, NOTHING.

HEY, GIRLS, LET'S PLAY TAG!

YOU'RE IT NOW, AMY.

YOU KNOW, AMY, IF YOU'RE TIRED OF PLAYING THOSE LITTLE GIRLS' GAMES, YOU CAN COME JOIN US.
OH, SURE, WHY NOT?

MAKE A LITTLE ROOM FOR MY FRIEND AMY. SHE, TOO, IS MIGHTY INTERESTED IN THE ADVENTURES OF HEROES!!

BY THE WAY, I FORGOT TO TELL YOU ABOUT THE PICNIC I'M HAV-ING AT MY HOME. I'M INVITING YOU, SALLY, AND YOU, TOO, GRACIE.
AM I INVITED, TOO? AND JOE?

ALL MY FRIENDS ARE, AND THOSE WHO'D LIKE TO BE.
AND ME?
AND ME?

DIING! DIING! DIING!
COME ON, CHILDREN, THAT'S ENOUGH PLAYING. IT'S TIME FOR YOUR SCHOOLING.

THAT'S GOOD, SALLY, YOU CAN STOP READING NOW.

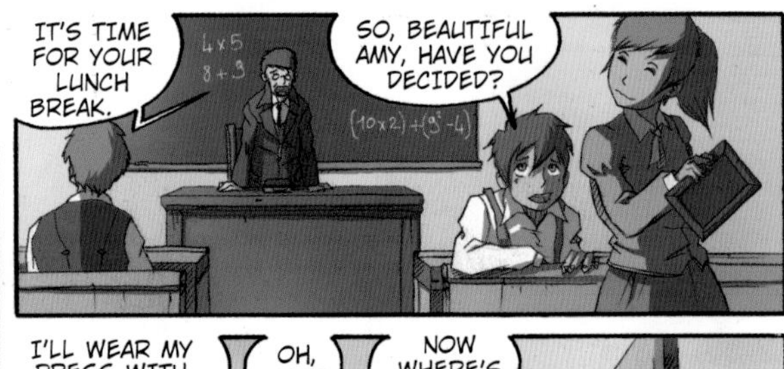
IT'S TIME FOR YOUR LUNCH BREAK.
SO, BEAUTIFUL AMY, HAVE YOU DECIDED?

I'LL WEAR MY DRESS WITH THE PINK RIBBONS.
OH, YES?
NOW WHERE'S BECKY?

IT LOOKS SO NICE ON ME.
SHE WON'T GET JEALOUS UNLESS SHE SEES ME WITH THIS SILLY THING...?

LOOK HOW CLEAR THIS ONE IS, BECKY.
OH!! YES, I LOVE THIS ONE. IT'S SO REFINED.
...

WE'LL TALK ABOUT ALL THAT LATER, AMY.

I JUST DON'T GET IT, JOE. THAT TREACHEROUS BECKY'S FLIRTING WITH ALFRED TEMPLE.
SO WHAT? I THOUGHT YOU DIDN'T CARE ABOUT HER?

THAT'S RIGHT, BUT THAT SHOW-OFF IS MY SWORN ENEMY.
YEAH, YEAH.
HE'S JEALOUS.

I LICKED HIM THE FIRST DAY HE EVER SAW THIS TOWN AND I'LL LICK HIM AGAIN.

THAT'S ENOUGH! I DON'T CARE FOR YOU OR YOUR PICTURES!
BUT BECKY! WHAT'S GOTTEN INTO YOU?

GO AWAY AND LEAVE ME ALONE, CAN'T YOU?! I HATE YOU!
I GET IT. YOU USED ME TO MAKE THAT CONCEITED TOM SAWYER JEALOUS!

BUT SHE WON'T GET AWAY WITH IT LIKE THAT. I'LL GET MY REVENGE ON YOUR "FIANCE" THERE. HE'LL BE PUNISHED GOOD, TRUST YOU ME.

♪

TOM, I'VE A NOTION TO SKIN YOU ALIVE!

AUNTIE, WHAT HAVE I DONE?
YOU KNOW FULL WELL. YOU LIED TO ME--HUMILIATED ME--AND MADE A FOOL OF ME WITH YOUR SO-CALLED DREAM.

I'VE JUST COME FROM MRS. HARPER'S, AND JOE HAD TOLD HER EVERYTHING: HOW YOU'D COME BACK HERE WEDNESDAY, HOW YOU'D DECIDED TO ONLY COME BACK ON SUNDAY SO THE SETTING WOULD BE PERFECT.

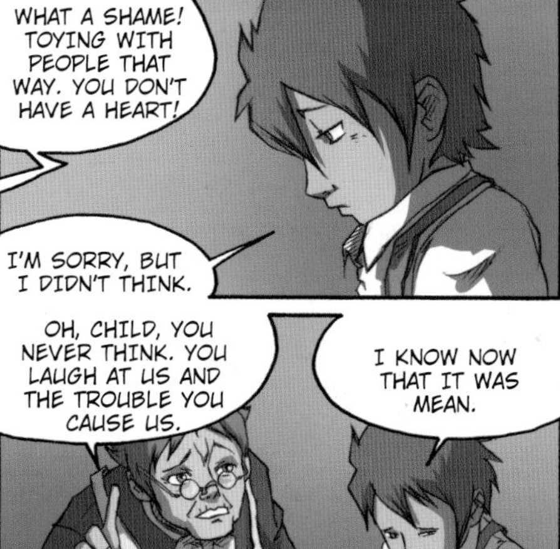
WHAT A SHAME! TOYING WITH PEOPLE THAT WAY. YOU DON'T HAVE A HEART!
I'M SORRY, BUT I DIDN'T THINK.
OH, CHILD, YOU NEVER THINK. YOU LAUGH AT US AND THE TROUBLE YOU CAUSE US.
I KNOW NOW THAT IT WAS MEAN.

WHY ALL THOSE LIES THEN?
I WANTED TO KEEP YOU FROM GRIEVING, THAT'S WHY I CAME TO LEAVE THE BARK, BUT I DIDN'T DARE LEAVE IT.

WHAT'S THIS STORY AGAIN ABOUT SOME BARK?

I'D WRITTEN A MESSAGE ON IT TO EASE YOUR MIND.
IT MUST STILL BE IN MY MUDDY BREECHES.

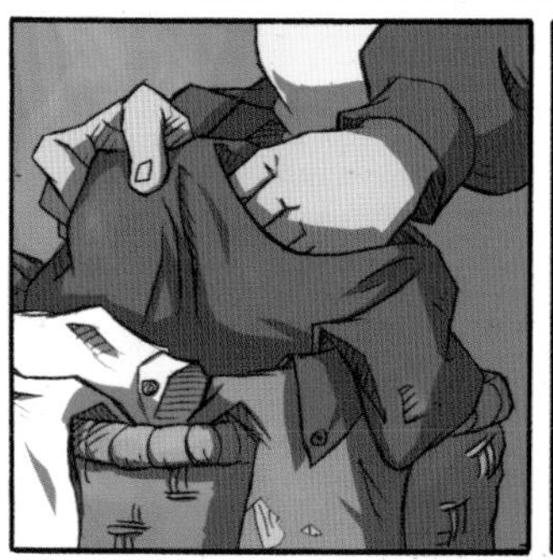

I RECKON HE'S LIED ABOUT IT--BUT IT'S A BLESSED, BLESSED LIE.

ALIVE DOING FINE SORRY
HE'S THE BEST, DIRTY, LITTLE BOY.

ANOTHER GOOD BREAKFAST. THE NEW COOK'S JUST GRAND...
BECKYYYYYYY!!

HEY, BECKY, WAIT UP!

I KNOW I WASN'T VERY NICE TO YOU THIS MORNING, BUT I'D LIKE TO MAKE UP. YOU'RE MY GIRLFRIEND.

KEEP YOURSELF TO YOURSELF, MR. THOMAS SAWYER.
I'LL NEVER SPEAK TO YOU AGAIN.

OHHH! IF YOU WERE A BOY, I'D TROUNCE YOU AND GIVE YOU A LICK-ING YOU WOULD-N'T FORGET ANY-TIME SOON!

YOU'RE JUST A DIRTY GIRL!
MAYBE, BUT WE'LL SEE JUST HOW LONG YOU GO ON PLAYING YOUR MISCHIEF.

OOOO, SHE'D BITE ME IF SHE HAD ANY TEETH. GRRRRR! I'M SO AFRAID!

MAKE FUN IF YOU WANT...
...JUST KNOW YOU'RE NOT THE ONLY ONE WHO CAN DO THAT.

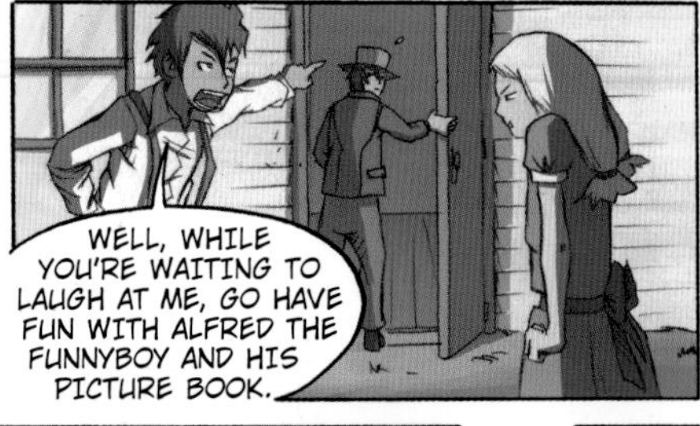
WELL, WHILE YOU'RE WAITING TO LAUGH AT ME, GO HAVE FUN WITH ALFRED THE FUNNYBOY AND HIS PICTURE BOOK.

PFFFFFFFFFF!!

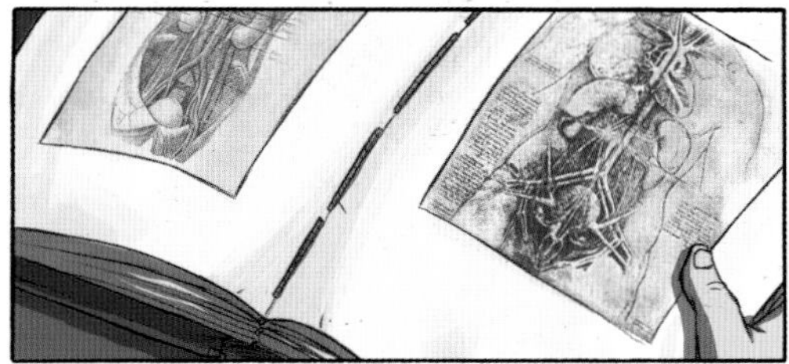

WHAT ARE YOU LOOKING AT?
!!

OH, NO.
SCCRRiiiiiTSCH

TOM SAWYER, YOU SEE WHAT HAPPENS WHEN YOU SPY ON FOLKS LIKE THAT!
HOW COULD I KNOW YOU'D TAKEN THE TEACHER'S SECRET BOOK, THE ONE HE LOOKS AT WHEN WE HAVE A TEST.

WHEN I CAME BY, I SAW THAT, FOR ONCE, HE'D LEFT THE KEY IN THE LOCK OF THE DRAWER.
I ADMIT I COULDN'T RESIST MY CURIOSITY.

AND NOW I'LL GET PUNISHED!
NOW YOU'RE GOING TO TELL ON ME, AND I'LL BE WHIPPED IN CLASS FOR THE FIRST TIME IN MY LIFE, ME WHO'S SUCH A GOOD STUDENT.

WHAT A CURIOUS KIND OF FOOL A GIRL IS. TO THINK THAT YOU'D NEVER BEEN LICKED AT OUR AGE.

IN ANY CASE, I'M NOT ONE TO BE A TATTLETALE, BUT IT'LL BE OBVIOUS SHE'S GUILTY. SHE'LL GET CAUGHT.

TOO BAD FOR HER. SHE HAD IT COMING.

THOMAS SAWYER, YOU COULD BE CONTENT WITH BEING A DUNCE, BUT NO, YOU HAVE TO BE A SLOB OF THE FIRST ORDER, TOO.
I DON'T REMEMBER DOING THAT. IT MUST'VE BEEN AN ACCIDENT.
THAT'S JUST YOUR PROBLEM: YOUR THOUGHTLESSNESS!

I KNOW THAT ALFRED DID THAT TO GET REVENGE ON TOM. IT'D BE EASY TO TURN IN THE REAL, GUILTY PARTY...

BUT SINCE HE'LL TELL ABOUT ME TEARING THE TEACHER'S PICTURE BOOK, I WON'T SAY A WORD!

A GOOD WHIPPING WILL SET YOUR MIND IN ORDER.

COME JOIN ME IN THE FRONT OF THE ROOM, PLEASE.

LET THAT SERVE AS A LESSON TO ALL OF YOU. I HOPE THAT, IN THE FUTURE, YOU'LL BE MUCH LESS NEGLIGENT WITH YOUR THINGS.

SO, AFTER THIS DIVERSION, LET'S FINALLY GET TO WORK.

EVERYONE STUDY SILENTLY. I DON'T WANT TO HEAR A PEEP!

WHAT?!!

WHO?!!
WHO TORE MY PRECIOUS BOOK?

I'M WAITING FOR THE GUILTY PARTY TO CONFESS!

BENJAMIN ROGERS, IS IT YOU?
NO, SIR.

JOSPEH HARPER, IS IT YOU?
NO, SIR.

AMY LAWRENCE?
NO, SIR.

REBECCA THATCHER? DID YOU TEAR THIS BOOK?
ANSWER ME!!!

NO! I DONE IT!

THIS TIME, MY LITTLE FRIEND, IS TOO MUCH!
YOU'LL REMEMBER THIS PUNISHMENT FOR A LONG TIME, BELIEVE ME.

"AND YOU CAN COUNT ON TWO BUSY HOURS OF BEING KEPT AFTER SCHOOL!"
IT WAS NICE OF YOU TO WAIT FOR ME, BECKY.
WAIT. YOU WERE THE ONE WHO WAS KIND TO HAVE TOLD ON YOURSELF IN MY PLACE.

AWW, I'M A BOY, MY SKIN'S HARD, IT'S NOT LIKE WITH YOU.
YOU DIDN'T HAVE TO DO IT. I WAS A COWARD. I DIDN'T SAY IT WAS ALFRED WHO SECRETLY SPILLED THE INKWELL ON YOUR BOOK.
AH, I'LL GET THAT SCOUNDREL BACK, AND IT'LL HURT!

DON'T DO THAT, TOM.

HEROES MUST NEVER LOWER THEMSELVES TO ACTING LIKE THEIR ENEMIES.

YOU KNOW, TIME'S ALL I'VE GOT LEFT. LET ME HAVE THE PLEASURE OF SPENDING IT WITH YOU.

IT GOT OFF TO A GOOD START.
WE'D FIGURED OUT A PLAN TO GET OUR REVENGE UPON MR. DOBBINS ON EXAMINATION DAY.

WE KNEW THAT EVERY YEAR HE GOT READY FOR THE EVENT BY SECRETLY HAVING A LITTLE DRINK OR TWO.

EACH ONE FOLLOWED THE OTHER ONTO THE PLATFORM, DOING THEIR LITTLE EXERCISES. BECKY'D PUT ON A PRETTY DRESS AND KNEW HER LINES PERFECTLY.

MY TURN CAME TO SAY MY RECITATION, AND I HAVE TO SAY I DID MY OWN LITTLE BIT.

JUST AS PLANNED, HE GOT UP TO FUSS. HE HAD A LITTLE TROUBLE STAYING STANDING UP. EVERYONE WAS WATCHING HIM AND STARTED TITTERING.

THEN IT WAS GINNY TOOFORD'S TURN TO DO HER EXERCISE. SHE WAS SUPPOSED TO PLAY LIKE SHE'D GOTTEN UPSET AND ANNOY THE TEACHER.

NOW'S WHEN EVERYTHING'S SUPPOSED TO GET STARTED! WE OPENED UP THE TRAP DOOR AND BEGAN LOWERING A CAT.

ITS CLAWS GRABBED MR. DOBBIN'S WIG, BARING HIS BALD PATE GILDED BY THE SIGN PAINTER'S SON DURING THE SCHOOLMASTER'S NAP!

IT WAS HILARIOUS, EVEN FOR THE PASTOR AND THE JUDGE.

WE BOYS WERE AVENGED.

LATER, A CIRCUS CAME AND SET UP ON THE TOWN GREEN.

WE HAD A GOOD TIME. THE SHOW WAS A FINE ONE.

AFTER THAT, WE PLAYED BEING TIGHTROPE WALKERS. I WAS A GREAT ACROBAT TAKING ENORMOUS RISKS!

AND A CLOWN, TOO, WHO MADE EVERYONE LAUGH.

BUT WITH BECKY LEAVING, THERE WAS NO BRIGHT SIDE TO LIFE ANYWHERE. SHE WAS GOING TO SPEND HER VACATION IN MISSOURI.

I'D REALLY LIKED TO HAVE ENJOYED ALL THIS FINE WEATHER WITH YOU.
ME, TOO, BUT LIFE SOMETIME COMES BETWEEN LOVED ONES.

BE STRONG. IT'LL FLY RIGHT BY.
AND DON'T FORGET ME!
I'D SEEN HER GO OFF WITHOUT BEING ABLE TO KEEP HER WITH ME.

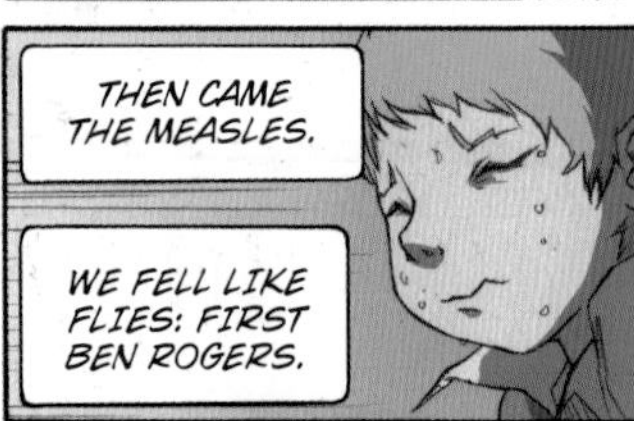
THEN CAME THE MEASLES.
WE FELL LIKE FLIES: FIRST BEN ROGERS.

THEN JOE.

THEN SID.

AND FINALLY IT WAS MY TURN.

EVEN IF IT WAS A LOT MORE SERIOUS FOR ME THAN THE OTHERS.

I TOOK TWO LONG WEEKS TO GET BETTER, BUT WHEN I TRIED TO GO SEE MY FRIENDS,
IT WAS HORRIBLE!!

THERE HAD BEEN A "REVIVAL," AND EVERYBODY HAD "GOT RELIGION!"

I TRIED TO SEE JOE, BUT HE COMPLETELY IGNORED ME, WITH HIS NOSE STUCK IN HIS BIBLE.

SO I LOOKED FOR BEN ROGERS, AND FOUND HIM VISITING THE POOR WITH A BASKET OF TRACTS.

I WAS DESPERATE, BUT I TOLD MYSELF THAT HUCK THE REBEL WOULD COMFORT ME!

WELL, NO, FOR HE, TOO, HAD BEEN TOUCHED BY GRACE!
COME ON, HUCK, LET'S GO PLAY PIRATES OR THE CIRCUS, WHAT-EVER YOU WANT.
SORRY, BUT I DON'T WANT TO BE A SINNER. I WON'T GO TO HELL.

YOU MUST BE AFRAID OF DIVINE ANGER, YOU KNOW. IN FACT, JUST LOOK: WE HAD EVIL THOUGHTS, AND A STORM'S COMING UP TO PUNISH US.

I WENT HOME WET, DISGUSTED, AND ALONE. AND THE TEMPEST LASTED ALL NIGHT.

BROOOMM!
I HAD NOT THE SHADOW OF A DOUBT IT WAS MY FAULT. I PRAYED FOR PROVIDENCE TO SPARE ME.

I DIDN'T GET STRUCK BY LIGHTNING, BUT WITH A RELAPSE. I SPENT THREE WEEKS ON MY BACK, STUFFED WITH POTIONS AND PILLS.

IN FACT, THIS IS MY FIRST TIME OUT.

WELL, MY BOY, THAT'S A MIGHTY SAD SUMMER VACATION INDEED.

IT MAKES ME HAPPY THAT YOU AIN'T FORGOT ME.
YOU CAN'T SAY I'M THE ONLY ONE WHO'S THINKING ABOUT YOU. HERE COMES HUCK.

BIRDS OF A FEATHER, SO THEY SAY.
OF THE BEST KIND, YOU MEAN!

I SEE YOU BROUGHT SOMETHING TO EAT. I GOT A LITTLE TOBACCO.

YOU'RE GOOD BOYS!

YOU'VE BEEN MIGHTY GOOD TO ME, BOYS.
ALWAYS READY TO HELP A WRETCH LIKE ME.

I DONE AN AWFUL THING--DRUNK AND CRAZY AT THE TIME--AND NOW I GOT TO SWING FOR IT, AND IT'S ONLY RIGHT.

PROMISE ME YOU WON'T EVER GET DRUNK!
PROMISE!

COME A LITTLE CLOSER, SO I CAN SEE THE GOOD, FRIENDLY FACES WHO'VE BEEN SO KIND TO OLD MUFF.

I HATE LIKE THE DICKENS SEEING HIM SO, WHEN HE NEVER DONE--THAT..
YEAH, ME, TOO.

HE'S CLEARLY NO ANGEL, BUT HE DON'T DESERVE THAT.
HE'S A GONER, THAT'S FOR SURE.

STILL, IT'S TOO BAD WE CAN'T DO ANYTHING TO SAVE HIM. HAVE YOU TOLD ANY-BODY ABOUT THAT?
'BOUT WHAT?

YOU KNOW WHAT!
OH--COURSE I HAVEN'T.

NEVER A WORD?
NEVER A SOLITARY WORD!

ARE YOU SURE?
OF COURSE, I AIN'T CRAZY. I REALLY DON'T WANT INJUN JOE TAKING TOO CLOSE AN INTEREST IN ME.

WHAT IF THEY TORTURED YOU?
NOBODY COULD EVER MAKE ME BREATHE A WORD.

BUT LET'S SWEAR AGAIN, ANYWAY. IT'S MORE SURER.
I'M AGREED.

WE SWEAR TO NEVER TALK ABOUT NOTHING. AND IF, EVEN UNDER TORTURE, SOMEONE MAKES THE TWO OF US TALK, THAT WITCHES FROM HELL WILL COME AND DRAG HIM AWAY BY HIS FEET TO THE DEVIL'S TABLE!
I SWEAR.

I'LL BE GLAD WHEN IT'S ALL OVER, I CAN'T GO ON LIKE THIS.
IN THE MEANTIME, MAYBE WE SHOULDN'T SEE EACH OTHER TOO MUCH.

I RECKON THAT MONSTER POTTER WILL SOON STOP HIS WRONGDOING.

THE TESTIMONY LEAVES NO DOUBT. HE'S A GONER.

WE'LL BE HAPPY ONCE YOU'RE DEAD, YOU OLD SCOUNDREL!

HEY! TOM, ARE YOU COMING TO PLAY WITH US?

I DON'T KNOW, I...

IF YOU WANT, YOU CAN PLAY THE SHERIFF'S PART.
COME ON, WE'LL HAVE A GOOD TIME.

OR PLAY THE JUDGE HIMSELF. YOU CAN DECIDE TO CONDEMN HIM.
THAT'S NOT FUNNY TO ME. MUFF POTTER'S GONNA BE HANGED.

THAT MEANS HE'S GONNA DIE, DON'T YOU UNDERSTAND?!

TOOOOOOM?!!

DON'T CRY, TOM.

IT'S ALL YOUR FAULT I GOT HANGED.

YOU'LL JUST HAVE TO LIVE WITH IT!!

IT'S NOT MY FAULT.
NOT MY FAULT.

IT'S JUST NOT RIGHT. I CAN'T LET THIS HAPPEN.

MEEOWWWWWW! MEEOOOOOWWWW!

YOU'VE REALLY GOT TO PRACTICE BEING A CAT, TOM.
LATER. COME ON DOWN!

YES, YOU'RE RIGHT.
SO, LET'S NOT WASTE ANY TIME!!

STILL, IT'S TOO RISKY!
COME ON, WE'RE NOT MARCHING!

I'VE NEVER BEEN IN SUCH A NICE HOUSE.
THERE'S ALWAYS A FIRST TIME.

LAW OFFICE

LADIES AND GENTLEMAN, THE COURT.

COURT IS NOW IN SESSION.
WE'LL START OFF BY HEARING FROM THE WITNESSES.

THAT'S WHEN I SAW MUFF POTTER WASHING OFF IN THE RIVER, THE SAME MORNING AS THE MURDER. WHEN I SPOKE TO HIM, HE RAN AWAY.

DOES THE DEFENSE COUNSEL HAVE ANY QUESTIONS?
NONE.

AND THAT'S HOW I FOUND THE KNIFE NEAR DOCTOR ROBINSON'S CORPSE.

I SAW THAT THERE KNIFE IN POTTER'S POSSESSION, AND MORE THAN ONCE!

ANY QUESTIONS, MR. JACKSON?
NONE. THE WITNESS MAY BE EXCUSED.

STILL NOW, THAT LAWYER...
HE'S NOT EVEN TRYING TO DEFEND POTTER.
I WOULDN'T WANT HIM, IF I HAD ANY PROBLEMS.

MEMBERS OF THE JURY, THE CITIZENS WHOM WE'VE JUST HEARD HAVE BROUGHT US THE PROOF THAT THIS CRIME IS INDEED THE WORK OF POTTER.

LET JUSTICE BE...
YOUR HONOR, A MOMENT, PLEASE, I HAVE A STATE-MENT TO MAKE.

IN OUR REMARKS AT THE OPENING OF THIS TRIAL, WE FORESHADOWED OUR PURPOSE TO PROVE THAT OUR CLIENT DID THIS FEARSOME DEED WHILE UNDER THE INFLUENCE OF A BLIND AND IRRE-SPONSIBLE DELIRIUM PRODUCED BY DRINK.

WE HAVE CHANGED OUR MIND. CLERK, CALL THOMAS SAWYER!

SILENCE IN THE COURT!

THOMAS SAWYER, DO YOU SWEAR ON THE BIBLE TO TELL THE WHOLE TRUTH?
I DO.

THOMAS SAWYER, WHERE WERE YOU ON THE 17TH OF JUNE, ABOUT THE HOUR OF MIDNIGHT?
IN THE GRAVEYARD, IN THE VAULT BESIDE HORSE WILLIAM'S GRAVE.

AND WHAT DID YOU SEE OF INTEREST TO THE COURT?
...

INJUN JOE'S THE ONE WHO KILLED THE DOCTOR WITH MUFF'S KNIFE!

JOE?!

ARREST HIM!!

GO AFTER HIM, FOR GOD'S SAKE!

AND BRING HIM TO ME!

YOU'RE DEAD!

HE'S...HE'S GOTTEN AWAY, YOUR HONOR.

YOU'LL SEE. I'LL TAKE GOOD CARE OF YOU, YOU STOOL PIGEON.
MUFF DIDN'T DESERVE THAT! HE HADN'T DONE NOTHING!

SING...

SING, LITTLE BLACKBIRD!

YOU'D BETTER, 'CAUSE I'M GONNA GET STARTED BY SLICING OUT YOUR TONGUE.

NAAARRRRRRRRRRRRRHHHHH!

THAT BLASTED INJUN JOE.

SO LONG AS HE AIN'T IN JAIL...

I DON'T RECKO I'LL EVER GET GOOD NIGHT'S SLEEP.

HOW ARE YOU DOING, TOM DEAR?

HERE, YOU BRAVE LITTLE FELLOW, SOMETHING SWEET. YOU DESERVE IT.

MY DELIV-ERER! HELLO!
HELLO.

SO, YOU'RE A CARPENTER NOW?
OH, YES, MISTER JASON WAS KIND ENOUGH TO HIRE ME ON.

IT'S ONLY RIGHT TO GIVE A HELP-ING HAND TO A GOOD FELLOW LIKE MUFF.
THAT'S RIGHT NICE OF YOU.

WELL, THIS IS NICE AND ALL, BUT WE'VE GOT A ROOF TO FINISH UP.
HAVE A GOOD DAY!

IT WAS A GOOD THING TELLING THE TRUTH. NOW EVERY-BODY LOVES MUFF, BUT IF I HADN'T SAID ANYTHING...

HUUUCKK!

I'M HERE, A-GETTING MY LUNCH.

OH, ARE THEY BITING?
LESS'N USUAL. THE FISH CAN TELL I'M ALL NERVOUS.

I HEAR YOU. IT'S THE SAME WITH ME.
IT'S BECAUSE OF INJUN JOE.

I HOPE THE SEARCH PARTIES WILL TURN UP SOMETHING.
THAT'D SPARE ME ALL THE TIME THINKING ON WHAT HE MIGHT DO TO ME. NIGHTTIME'S EVEN WORSE.

DETECTIVES, REWARDS, WANTED POSTERS...YOU GOT TO HOPE!!
HONEST, I THINK I'D JUST AS WELL SEE HIM DEAD.

WE OUGHT TO GET STARTED ON SOME GRAND PROJECT FOR A CHANGE OF MIND.
REALLY.

WHAT IF WE STARTED OUR PIRATE GAMES AGAIN. LOOK AT MY NEW SWORD.
NO, WE NEED SOMETHING EVEN BETTER.

WAIT, I HAVE A FABULOUS IDEA.
OH, YEAH? WHAT'S THAT?

WE'RE GONNA GO ON A TREASURE HUNT!

THAT'S FINE, BUT WHERE DO WE FIND TREASURE?
OH, MOST ANY-WHERE.

WHY, IS IT HID ALL AROUND?
NO, INDEED IT AIN'T.
IT'S HID IN MIGHTY PAR-TICULAR PLACES, AND THEY LEAVE MARKS ON OLD YELLOW PAPER.

WHO'S "THEY"?
WHY, ROB-BERS, OF COURSE.

THEN WHY DO THEY HIDE IT INSTEAD OF SPENDING IT?
I DON'T KNOW, THAT'S JUST HOW IT IS!
DON'T THEY COME AFTER IT ANY MORE?

THEY MEAN TO, BUT THE PAPER GETS STOLEN, OR ELSE THEY DIE.
ANYWAY, THE TREASURE'S JUST WAITING TO BE FOUND.
SO HOW'S SOMEBODY GONNA DO THAT?

IT'S SIMPLE, BY AND BY SOMEBODY FINDS THE OLD YELLOW PAPER, WITH HY'RO-GLYPHICS AND ALL THE MARKS.
HYRO-WHICH?
HY'ROGLIPHICS PICTURES AND THINGS, YOU KNOW, THAT DON'T SEEM TO MEAN ANYTHING.
HAVE YOU GOT ONE OF THEM PAPERS, TOM?

WELL, NO...
...YOU DON'T JUST FIND 'EM LYING ALL OVER THE PLACE.
WELL, THEN, HOW YOU GOING TO FIND THE MARKS?

I DON'T WANT ANY MARKS. THEY ALWAYS BURY IT UNDER A HAUNTED HOUSE OR UNDER A DEAD TREE.
I KNOW AN OLD DEAD-LIMB TREE NOT FAR FROM HERE!

WE'LL START WITH IT. AND IF WE DON'T FIND NOTHING, WE'LL GO ALL THE WAY TO THE HAUNTED HOUSE.
THIS IS HARD WORK!
YEAH BUT...
FORTUNE BELONGS TO THOSE WHO KILL THEMSELVES BY DIGGING TOO MUCH.

IF WE FIND TREASURE HERE, I'LL HAVE PIE AND A GLASS OF SODA EVERY DAY.
I'LL HAVE A GREAT TIME.

I'LL SAVE MY PART FOR WHEN I'M MARRIED.

THAT'S THE FOOLISHEST THING YOU COULD DO.
WHY'S THAT?

LOOK AT PAP AND MOTHER. FIGHT! WHY, THEY USED TO FIGHT ALL THE TIME.

THAT AIN'T ANYTHING. THE GIRL I'M GOING TO MARRY WON'T FIGHT.

WHAT'S THE NAME OF THE GAL?
IT AIN'T A GAL AT ALL-- IT'S A GIRL.

TOM, I RECKON THEY'RE ALL ALIKE. THEY'LL ALL COMB A BODY.
YOU'RE JUST BEING NEGATIVE.

ONLY IF YOU GET MARRIED, I'LL BE MORE LONESOMER THAN EVER.

NO, YOU WON'T. YOU'LL COME AND LIVE WITH ME!

HMM...

OTHERWISE, DO YOU RECKON THERE'S REALLY ANY TREASURE HERE?
I DOUBT IT. ANYWAY, THERE CAN'T BE SOME AT THE FOOT OF EVERY DEAD TREE. IT'D BE TOO EASY!

COME ON, LET'S HEAD TO THE NEXT ONE.

THAT'S THE FIFTH ONE AND STILL NO TREASURE.
I RECKON MAYBE WE'LL TACKLE THE OLD TREE THAT'S OVER YONDER ON CARDIFF HILL BACK OF THE WIDOW'S.

BUT WON'T THE WIDOW TAKE IT AWAY FROM US, TOM? IT'S ON HER LAND.
I'D LIKE TO SEE THAT. WHOEVER FINDS ONE OF THESE HID TREASURES, IT BELONGS TO HIM.

BLAME IT, WE MUST BE IN THE WRONG PLACE AGAIN.
SOMETIMES WITCHES INTERFERE. I RECKON MAYBE THAT'S WHAT'S THE TROUBLE NOW.

SHUCKS, WITCHES AIN'T GOT NO POWER IN THE DAYTIME.
WELL, THAT'S SO. OH, I KNOW WHAT THE MATTER IS! YOU GOT TO FIND WHERE THE SHADOW OF THE LIMB FALLS AT MIDNIGHT.

WHAT?
WE DID ALL THAT FOR NOTHING AND WE HAVE TO COME BACK IN THE NIGHT?
WE HAVE TO! COME MEOW UNDER MY WINDOW AROUND 11 O'CLOCK, AND WE'LL COME BACK.

NOTHING STILL.

WELL, BUT WE CAN'T BE WRONG. WE SPOTTED THE SHADOW TO A DOT.
MAYBE IT WEREN'T EXACTLY MIDNIGHT.
I FEEL LIKE SOMEBODY'S WATCHING ME AND I DON'T LIKE WITCHES AND GHOSTS A-FLUTTERING AROUND SO.
AND THEY MOST ALWAYS PUT IN A DEAD MAN WHEN THEY BURY A TREASURE UNDER A TREE, TO LOOK OUT FOR IT.

LET'S GET OUT OF HERE.
ALL RIGHT. LET'S HIDE THE TOOLS IN THE BUSHES AND WE'LL FETCH 'EM TOMORROW AND GO TO THE HAUNTED HOUSE.

LOOKY-HERE, TOM, DO YOU KNOW WHAT DAY IT IS?
FRIDAY!!!

I NEVER ONCE THOUGHT OF IT, HUCK!
THERE'S SOME LUCKY DAYS, MAYBE, BUT FRIDAY AIN'T. AND I DREAMT ABOUT RATS.

NO! SURE SIGN OF TROUBLE.
SERIOUS.

A GOOD TREASURE HUNTER MUST HAVE LUCK ON HIS SIDE. AND HERE ALL THE SIGNS OF FATE ARE TOTALLY AGAINST US.
THAT'S CLEAR.

WE'LL DROP THIS THING FOR TODAY, AND PLAY.
YEAH, AND THAT'LL REST OUR BLISTERS.

DO YOU KNOW ROBIN HOOD, HUCK?
IS HE A FRIEND OF YOURS?

AN IMAGINARY ONE. AN ENGLISH PRINCE OF ROBBERS, WHO TOOK FROM THE RICH TO GIVE TO THE POOR.
WELL, HE MUST HAVE BEEN A GOOD FELLOW.
HE WAS THE NOBLEST MAN THAT EVER WAS! AND HE COULD PLUG A TEN-CENT PIECE WITH A SINGLE ARROW.
A FELLOW WHO'S GOOD IN A TUSSLE!

THAT'S JUST DANDY, I'VE GOT SOME STRING. LET'S MAKE US A BOW!

YEAH, AND WE'LL LEARN TO FIRE WITH ONE HAND TIED BEHIND US, LIKE THAT FELLOW ROBIN.

IT AIN'T BEEN NO USE DIGGING ALL DAY, NOTHIN' STILL.

YOU SURE ARE LOOKING FOR TROUBLE! FIRST DEAD MEN, NOW YOU'RE TALKING GHOSTS!
YOU RECKON? THOSE ARE ALL JUST STORIES TO KEEP FOLKS FROM GOING IN AND FINDING THE TREASURE.
BUT A DEAD TREE IN FRONT OF A HAUNTED HOUSE ON AN ISLAND, IT SEEMED PERFECT!
WANT TO TAKE A LOOK INSIDE?

YOU'RE RIGHT, WE'RE NOT YELLOW BELLIES!
ALL RIGHT, LET'S GO IN.

NOTHING HERE. WANT TO LOOK UPSTAIRS?

IT'S THE OWNERS' GHOSTS COME BACK TO PUNISH US FOR BREAKING INTO THEIR HOME!
WE SAID WE'D STOP BELIEVING IN SUCH FOOL-ISHNESS.
NOBODY CAN KNOW ABOUT OUR PLAN.

I AIN'T OF A MIND TO BE CONDEMNED TO DEATH A SECOND TIME.
THAT'S...
INJUN JOE!!!
HA HA HA HA!!

THIS HOUSE AIN'T HAUNTED, JUST ABAN-DONED.
IT'S A MIGHTY STRANGE FEELING GOING INTO FOLKS' HOME WHO'VE MAYBE BEEN DEAD FOR YEARS.

WE'LL HAVE A CHANCE TO TALK HERE.
VOICES, DOWNSTAIRS!

YOUR SAME OLD STORY.
WE'D DO BETTER TO CLEAR ON OUT OF HERE RIGHT QUICK WITH OUR LOOT, AND GO LIVE IT UP SOMEWHERE ELSE.
NO WAY, BUSINESS IS BUSINESS!
THEN FOR TEXAS! WE'LL LEG IT TOGETHER!

IN THE MEANTIME, I'M DEAD FOR SLEEP! IT'S YOUR TURN TO WATCH.
AND TRY NOT TO FALL ASLEEP LIKE USUAL.
YES, BOSS.

ZZZZ
WHEN I KEEP WATCH...

I KEEP...

THEY'RE DEAD ASLEEP.
ZZZZ
ZZZZ

COME!
NOW'S OUR CHANCE.

CKRAAK!!
A NOISE?!!
THE TREASURE!!

NOBODY...
IT WAS JUST A BAD DREAM.
ZZZZ

ARRRRRRRRRRR!
HERE! YOU'RE A WATCHMAN, AIN'T YOU! YOU DIDN'T EVEN HEAR ME HOLLER.

THAT WAS A CLOSE CALL!
YOU GOT THAT RIGHT.
HAVE I BEEN ASLEEP?
OH, PARTLY, PARTLY.

LOOK HERE, YOU GO BACK UP THE RIVER, AND I'LL TAKE THE CHANCES ON DROPPING INTO TOWN FOR A LOOK.

WHAT DO WE DO WITH THE MONEY?
SIX HUNDRED AND FIFTY IN SILVER'S SOMETHING TO CARRY. AND NONE TOO DISCREET.

WE'LL JUST REGULARLY BURY IT AND COME FOR IT IN THE NIGHT.
YEAH, GOOD IDEA. GO FETCH IT.

COME, MY LITTLE DARLINGS, COME TO PAPA.
STOP ACTING THE FOOL, AND LET'S FIND A PLACE TO DIG.

WHAT LUCK!!
WE'VE FOUND OUR TREASURE.
YEAH, WE'RE GONNA BE RICH.

HELLO! A HALF-ROTTEN PLANK.
NO, IT'S A BOX.

MAN, IT'S MONEY!

HEY, THAT'S OUR HOLE!!

WE'LL GET IT OUT OF THERE. I SAW AN OLD PICKAX NEAR THE FIREPLACE.
TWAS ALWAYS SAID THAT MURREL'S GANG USED TO BE AROUND HERE. THIS MUST BE THEIR STASH.

PARD, THERE'S THOUSANDS OF DOLLARS HERE.
SHUCKS! IF THEY'D ONLY GOTTEN HERE TEN MINUTES LATER.

NOW YOU WON'T NEED TO DO THAT JOB.
NEVER! IT'S REVENGE!
BUT SOMETHING'S BOTHERING ME ALL THE SUDDEN.
THAT PICK HAD FRESH EARTH ON IT! THAT MEANS SOMEONE CAME AND MADE THESE HOLES JUST BEFORE US.
BURYING THE LOOT HERE'S TOO RISKY. WE'LL TAKE IT TO HIDEOUT NUMBER TWO.
WHO COULD HAVE BROUGHT THESE TOOLS HERE?
DO YOU RECKON THEY CAN BE UPSTAIRS?
OH, NO!
BY THE GREAT SACHEM!
CRAAC
WHOEVER HOVE THOSE THINGS IN HERE TOOK US FOR GHOSTS OR DEVILS AND RAN AWAY.
YOU'RE PROBABLY RIGHT. LET'S GO!
THAT WAS MIGHTY CLOSE!
YES. IT'S BAD LUCK WE DIDN'T THINK TO PUT THE TOOLS AWAY. BUT FOR THAT, INJUN JOE NEVER WOULD HAVE SUSPECTED.
THEY'RE FAR ENOUGH AWAY. WE CAN HEAD BACK.
LET'S TAKE THE MOST SECRETEST PATH. WE'D BETTER AVOID ANY CHANCE MEETINGS.
WE'LL HAVE TO KEEP A LOOKOUT FOR THAT SPANIARD.
AND FOLLOW HIM TO "NUMBER TWO"!
REVENGE? WHAT IF HE MEANS US?
DON'T SAY THAT.
IT'S TOO HORRIBLE!

YIPPEE!!

HEY, LOTS OF COINS HAVE FALL-EN INTO THE WATER!

WE DON'T CARE! WE'VE GOT PLENTY MORE.

UH...

JUST A DREAM. THIS HAS GOT TO HAPPEN FOR REAL.

LET'S GO FIND HUCK!

IF WE'D 'A' LEFT THE BLAME TOOLS AT THE DEAD TREE, WE'D 'A' GOT THE MONEY.

IF THEM STAIRS HADN'T BROKE DOWN, WE'D BE DEAD BY INJUN JOE'S HANDS RIGHT THIS VERY MINUTE.

YEAH, YOU'RE RIGHT. I'VE GOT NO DESIRE TO SEE THOSE TWO SCOUNDRELS AGAIN, BUT I WISH I UNDERSTOOD BETTER THAT THING ABOUT "NUMBER TWO."
MAYBE IT'S THE NUMBER OF A ROOM IN A TAVERN?

OH, THAT'S THE TRICK! THEY AIN'T ONLY TWO TAVERNS IN TOWN.

ALL RIGHT!
YOU STAY HERE, HUCK, TILL I COME.

ROOM NO. 2?

IT'S LONG BEEN OCCUPIED BY A YOUNG LAWYER. YOU'LL FIND HIM IN HIS OFFICE AT THIS HOUR.
THANK YOU, MISTER DENNIS.

TOO CLEAN HERE, AND A YOUNG LAWYER JUST AIN'T LIKELY.

HERE'S THE SECOND ONE... THAT SEEMS MORE LIKE IT.

HELLO, MARTIN, YOUR PA'S NOT HERE?
HE SAID HE HAD A MEETING, BUT HE'S REALLY JUST TAKING A NAP.

DO YOU KNOW WHETHER THERE'S ANYONE IN NO. 2?
OH, THAT ROOM'S A MYSTERY. IT'S KEPT LOCKED, BUT YOU NEVER SEE ANYBODY GO INTO IT OR COME OUT OF IT...
EXCEPT AT NIGHT.

TO MY MIND, IT'S HAUNTED, THAT'S ALL.
IN FACT, I'VE NOTICED A FUNNY LIGHT AND SHAD-OWS IN THERE.

THAT'S WHAT I FOUND OUT, HUCK. IT'S TAK-ING PLACE AT LAWSON'S.
NOW WHAT YOU GOING TO DO?

THAT NO. 2 HAS TWO WAYS IN, THE ONE ON THE MAIN STREET AND ONE ONTO AN ALLEY. THAT'S HOW WE'LL GET IN.
WE'LL TRY TO OPEN IT WITH ALL THE KEYS WE GET HOLD OF.

BUT WE GOT TO BE CAREFUL ABOUT JOE GETTING HIS REVENGE!
THAT'S WHY, IF WE DON'T GET THE DOOR OPEN, YOU'LL KEEP A LOOKOUT FOR INJUN JOE. AND IF YOU SEE HIM, YOU JUST FOLLOW HIM QUIET LIKE.

YOU GOT NOTHING TO FEAR, IT'LL BE NIGHT, SURE. JUST THINK ABOUT THE MONEY!

GOODNIGHT, PA!
GOODNIGHT, MARTIN.

MEEOOWW! MEEOOWW!

MEEOOWW! MEEOOWW!
YOU DO A RIGHT PURTY CAT!

IT'S GOOD, EVERYONE'S ASLEEP.
PASS ME THE KEYS YOU FOUND SO WE CAN GO AND TRY TO OPEN THAT DOOR.

YOU KEEP WATCH, AND AT THE SLIGHTEST HITCH, YOU MEOW.

GRR...
THAT ONE DON'T WORK EITHER!

OOPS...

IT WAS ALREADY OPEN.

!!!

ZZZZZZZZZZ
>GRFL!<

RUN FOR YOUR LIFE!

DID YOU SEE A GHOST OR WHAT?!
WORSE, INJUN JOE AS DRUNK AS A SKUNK.

BUT INJUN JOE, ALL THE SAME.
SAY, TOM, DID YOU SEE THAT BOX?

NOW'S A MIGHTY GOOD TIME TO GET THAT BOX, IF INJUN JOE'S DRUNK.
YOU'RE A BOLD ONE, HUCK.

I THINK HE'D ONLY DRUNK ONE KEG, IF THERE'D BEEN THREE, I'D DO IT. HE'S STILL DANGEROUS FOR NOW.

ALL RIGHT, I'LL KEEP AN EYE OUT DAY AND NIGHT. ONCE THERE'S ANY-THING NEW, I'LL COME A-MEOWING UNDER YOUR WINDOW.

SO, CHILDREN, HOW WILL YOU SPEND YOUR DAY?
I'M GOING TO 'TEND TO THE HOUSEWORK. THERE'S LOADS OF THINGS TO BE DONE.
COME NOW, GO OUTSIDE AND ENJOY THE SUNLIGHT. IT'LL DO YOU GOOD.
GOOD IDEA! I'LL GET SOME SUN WHILE FISHING.
I'D PLANNED ON GOING TO THE HOSPITAL WITH ALFRED AND THE GIRLS.
THAT'S A FUNNY WAY TO SPEND YOUR TIME, SID.
SPEAKING OF GIRLS, I HEARD AT THE GROCER'S YESTERDAY THAT THE THATCHERS ARE BACK IN TOWN.
HEY, I PLUMB FORGOT.
I'VE GOT SOMETHING MIGHTY IMPORTANT TO DO!
OH, YEAH? I WONDER WHAT THAT COULD BE.
WHO ASKED YOU...
DON'T FORGET TO WASH YOUR MOUTH OFF.
"MILK-STACHES" AREN'T OFTEN MENTIONED IN ROMANCE BOOKS.
YOUR INVITATION'S MADE ME SO VERY HAPPY. I'VE BEEN PINING FOR THIS PICNIC SINCE THE BEGINNING OF SUMMER VACATION.
WHAT'S MORE, PAPA HAS ORGANIZED A BOAT RIDE.
WHAT LUCK! A BOAT ALL TO OURSELVES!
HEY, THERE'S TOM.
TOM, YOU AND SID WILL BE COMING, WON'T YOU?
COMING WHERE?
TO THE PICNIC, OF COURSE. WE'LL BE GOING ALL THE WAY TO THE CREEK ON THE STEAM FERRYBOAT.
OH, IF WE'RE TAKING A RIDE ON THE RIVER, THE BLACK AVENGER OF THE JUETILLES IS YOUR MAN!
WE'LL HAVE A NICE TIME, YOU'LL SEE.

I'M HAPPY TO SEE YOU AGAIN. I MISSED YOU, YOU KNOW!
YES, AND NOW WE'LL ALWAYS BE TOGETHER!
IT SEEMED LIKE A LONG TIME TO ME, TOO, BUT TOMORROW WILL BE FUN!
FOR SURE, BECKY.
ALWAYS.

AH, IF WE FOUND THE TREASURE, HOW ASTONISHED BECKY'D BE.
WELL, HUCK OBVIOUSLY WON'T BE COMING TO LOOK FOR ME TONIGHT.

IT'S ALREADY LATE.
OR EARLY.

FALLING ILL AT THE HOSPITAL, HOW IRONIC. THERE'S NO WAY YOU'LL BE GOING ANYWHERE TODAY.
BUT, I PROMITH, I FEEL BETTER.

DON'T YOU WORRY, I'LL HAVE FUN ENOUGH FOR TWO!
THAT'S NOT VERY NICE, TOM.

YOU'LL NOT GET BACK TILL LATE. PERHAPS YOU'D BETTER STAY ALL NIGHT WITH SOME OF THE GIRLS, BECKY DEAR.
THEN I'LL STAY WITH SUSY HARPER, MAMMA.

VERY WELL, IT'S TIME TO GET GOING.

GOODBYE, MAMMA!
I'VE GOT AN IDEA, BECKY.

'STEAD OF GOING TO SUSY'S, WE'LL SLEEP OVER AT THE WIDOW DOUGLAS'S. SHE'LL HAVE ICE CREAM! SHE'LL BE AWFUL GLAD TO HAVE US.
OH, THAT WILL BE FUN!

DOES THAT MEAN I HAVE TO LIE TO MAMMA?
BUT SHUCKS! YOUR MOTHER WON'T KNOW. AND I BET YOU SHE'D 'A' SAID GO THERE IF SHE'D 'A' THOUGHT OF IT.

YOU'RE PROBABLY RIGHT.
DON'T WORRY.

NOTHING BAD WILL HAPPEN.

NOT LIKE THAT, MAN.
LET ME SHOW YOU.

I NAME THIS PLACE "TOMERICA!"
WHEEE!
YIPPEE!

TIME TO EAT!!!!
THAT WAS MIGHTY BOLD CALLING ME SCRAWNY, SUSY.
I DIDN'T SAY SCRAWNY.
THAT'S RIGHT. SHE SAID "SKINNY."
THAT'S THE SAME!!
OH, WHATEVER, WHAT COUNTS IS THAT I GUESSED IT WAS YOU.
GO ON, YOU POOR SPORT.

WHATEVER I'M TOUCHING FEELS ALL SKINNY.
IT WOULDN'T BE BEN ROGERS BY ANY CHANCE?

CAN WE HAVE A LITTLE MORE LEMONADE?
Y'ALL ARE RAVENOUS!
HEE! HEE!
AND SOME MORE OF THAT DEE-LICIOUS CHICKEN?
IT AIN'T OUR FAULT. IT'S GROWING PAINS!

WHO'S READY FOR THE CAVE?
GOOD IDEA!
ISN'T THAT DANGEROUS FOR CHILDREN?
NOT AT ALL, WE'LL STICK TOGETHER.
AND EVERYONE TAKE TWO CANDLES EACH! JUST IN CASE...

IT'S THAT WAY. WE HAVE TO HEAD UP THE HILL FIRST!

THE DOOR'S NOT LOCKED, JUST STUCK SHUT.
WAIT, WE'LL GET IT OPEN.
HEY, DON'T SNUFF OUT MY CANDLE!!
OOOOH, IT'S MARVELOUS.
HA HA HA!
DOES EVERYONE HAVE THEIR CANDLES?
MCDOUGAL'S CAVE IS TRULY A MAZE, THAT'S WHY IT'S BEEN A HIDEOUT FOR CRIMINALS.
WE SURE COULD FIND SOME TREASURES HERE.
BUT TO FIND ANY, YOU'VE GOT TO HAVE EITHER LOTS OF LUCK OR LOTS OF TIME.
WHAT A SHOWOFF. HE WEARS ME OUT WITH HIS BLATHERING ON.
OH! YOU'RE EXAGGERAT-ING.
DON'T YOU TRUST YOUR TOM?
YES, OF COURSE I DO.
LET'S GO THIS WAY.
DON'T YOU THINK THAT'S A LITTLE DAN-GEROUS?
DING! DING!
DOESN'T THAT SOUND LIKE A BELL?
IT'S THE SIGNAL FROM THE BOAT.
COME ON EVERYONE, WE'RE HEADING BACK.
IT'S CLOUDING OVER SOMETHING TERRIBLE. WE DON'T HAVE A MOMENT TO LOSE.
HANG ON, IT'S GOING TO GET ROUGH!

I WISH IT WAS ME ON THAT FERRYBOAT.

ALL RIGHTY, NOW LET'S TAKE A GANDER.

AH, THAT DIDN'T TAKE LONG.
AIN'T NO TIME TO WARN TOM, SO I'LL FOLLOW 'EM.

THEY MUST BE GONNA HIDE THE BOX IN THE CLEARING. THEY'RE GOING BY THE WIDOW DOUGLAS'S.

NO, THEY'VE DISAP-PEARED!

I'LL NEVER FIND 'EM AGAIN IN THIS STORM. I MIGHT AS WELL GO HOLE UP AT THE WIDOW DOUGLAS'S. SHE'S ALWAYS KIND TO M...
KOF KOF KOF

THIS WEATH-ER'S MADE ME CATCH A COLD.
SHUT UP!
DON'T GET US CAUGHT.

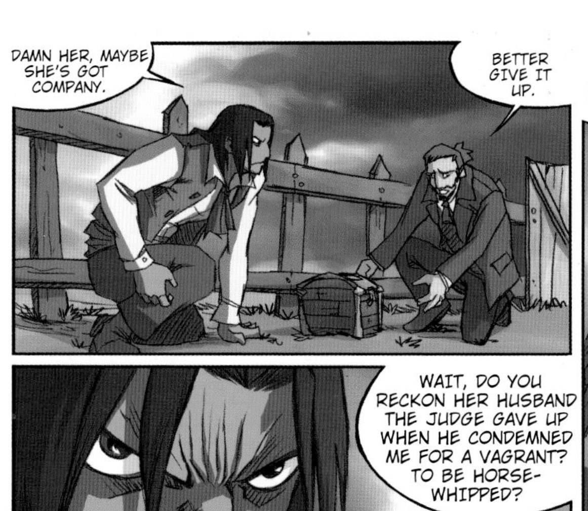
DAMN HER, MAYBE SHE'S GOT COMPANY.
BETTER GIVE IT UP.

OH, DON'T KILL HER!

BY GOD, THAT'S--
IF YOU DON'T HELP ME OVERPOWER HER, IT'S NOTHING COMPARED TO WHAT I'LL DO TO YOU.

WAIT, DO YOU RECKON HER HUSBAND THE JUDGE GAVE UP WHEN HE CONDEMNED ME FOR A VAGRANT? TO BE HORSE-WHIPPED?
HE TOOK ADVANTAGE OF ME AND DIED. BUT I'LL TAKE IT OUT OF HER.
WHEN YOU WANT TO GET REVENGE ON A WOMAN, YOU GO FOR HER LOOKS. YOU SLIT HER NOSTRILS YOU NOTCH HER EARS LIKE A SOW!

THE QUICKER THE BETTER.
DO IT NOW? AND COMPANY THERE? ARE YOU CRAZY?
WE'LL WAIT TILL THEY'RE GONE.

I CAN'T LET THIS HAPPEN. IT'S TOO AWFUL.

OPEN UP! HURRY!
HELP!
BLAM! BLAM!

IT AIN'T A NAME TO OPEN MANY DOORS.
BY GEORGE, HE HAS GOT SOME-THING TO TELL, OR HE WOULDN'T ACT SO.
WHO IS IT?
HUCKLEBERRY FINN--QUICK LET ME IN!
OVER AT THE WIDOW DOUGLAS'S, THAT KIND LADY, THERE'S SOME DANGEROUS ARMED MEN MEANING TO HARM HER.

COME ON BOYS, THERE'S NO TIME TO LOSE. GRAB YOUR RIFLES AND LET'S GO
PLEASE DON'T EVER TELL I TOLD YOU. I'D BE KILLED, SURE. YOU'LL KEEP IT SECRET, WON'T YOU?

EH?!
PROMISE!

OOOO!!

YOU'RE SO FOOLISH, TOM! I WAS FRIGHTENED.

HEY, LOOK, PEOPLE'S NAMES.

A TIM "THE CLEVER."
SURELY, THAT'S HIS DAD'S FIRST NAME.
AARON AND ALEXANDRA ROGERS, DO YOU RECKON THOSE ARE BEN'S PARENTS?
HERE'S SOMETHING ELSE: THOMAS S, THE INVINCIBLE PIRATE.
HA HA HA, A RIVAL.

COME ON, PIRATE OF MINE. LET'S WRITE SOMETHING, TOO.
Becky + Tom
WE WERE RIGHT TO LEAVE THE OTHERS. WE'RE HAVING MORE FUN BY OURSELVES, AIN'T WE?

YES, AND IT'S MAGNIFICENT, TOO! LOOK, CRYSTAL FLOWERS.
IT'S LIKE THE NIAGARA FALLS.

NOT QUITE, IT'S SMALLER.
OF COURSE, BUT WHAT A FALL.

HERE, PRINCESS.

THANKS, TOM.

RUN, MY DARLING, RUN!
FOLLOW ME QUIETLY.
WHAT?
AHRR!
THAT WAS HORRIBLE!
DON'T WORRY, IT'S OVER NOW.
SNIFF!
ATCHOO!
WE'VE BEEN SPOTTED, LET'S RUN.
IT'S TOO LONG!
DON'T FRET, IT'LL SOON BE TIME.
FIRE! FIRE!!
?!!
POW!
POW!
POW!

I WONDER HOW LONG WE'VE BEEN DOWN HERE, TOM. WE BETTER START BACK.
PERHAPS WE BETTER, BUT...

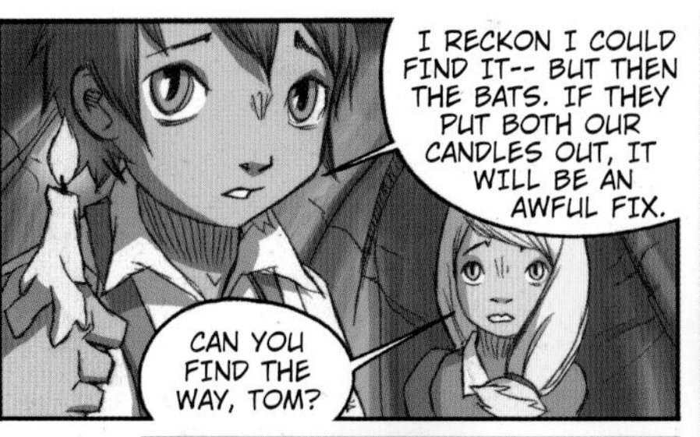
I RECKON I COULD FIND IT-- BUT THEN THE BATS. IF THEY PUT BOTH OUR CANDLES OUT, IT WILL BE AN AWFUL FIX.
CAN YOU FIND THE WAY, TOM?

LET'S TRY SOME OTHER WAY.
WELL. BUT I HOPE WE WON'T GET LOST.

WE'LL BE OUT SOON, DON'T WORRY.
I TRUST YOU!

YOU SAVED MY LIFE.
WE ONLY DID OUR DUTY, MA'AM.

IT WAS PROVIDENCE THAT SET YOU ON THE WAY TO MY HOUSE.
PROVIDENCE SPEAKS WITH MANY VOICES, YOU KNOW. SOMEONE CAME TO WARN US OF THE EMERGENCY.

VERY WELL! WILL YOU TELL ME WHO MY BENEFACTOR IS?
IMPOSSIBLE, HE DON'T ALLOW ME TO TELL HIS NAME.

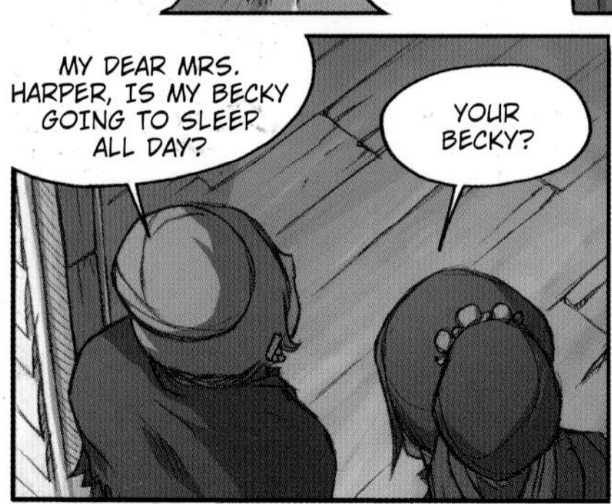
MY DEAR MRS. HARPER, IS MY BECKY GOING TO SLEEP ALL DAY?
YOUR BECKY?

YES, DIDN'T SHE STAY WITH YOU LAST NIGHT?
WHY, NO.

I'VE GOT A BOY THAT'S TURNED UP MISSING. I RECKON MY TOM STAYED AT YOUR HOUSE LAST NIGHT --ONE OF YOU.
HE DIDN'T STAY WITH US. LET'S ASK MY JOE.

JOE HARPER, HAVE YOU SEEN MY TOM THIS MORNING?
NO'M.
WHEN DID YOU SEE HIM LAST?
IT'S WHEN HE SAID HE'D HAD ENOUGH OF THAT SHOWOFF. WE WERE IN THE CAVE.
IT WAS DARK WHEN WE GOT BACK IN THE FERRYBOAT, WE WERE TIRED AND NO ONE THOUGHT OF COUNTING THE CHILDREN.
IT'S NOT POSSIBLE!
MAYBE THEY'RE STILL IN THE CAVE.
WE MUST GO BACK THERE AND START A SEARCH!
YES, TIME'S RUNNING OUT!
THE POOR CHILDREN!
WOO HOO!
IT'S TRUE. I'M ALL MIXED UP. I CAN'T FIND MY GUIDE MARKS.
COME HELP US!
WE'RE HERE!!
IT'S HORRID, WE'RE LOST.
COME, BE BRAVE. WE'LL GET OUT OF HERE IN THE END.
DO YOU SWEAR?
OF COURSE. IN THE MEANTIME, REST SOME, YOU'LL NEED YOUR STRENGTH.

ARE YOU READY, BOYS?
ARE YOU COMING WITH US, HUCK?

TOO LITTLE SLEEP, LITTLE FELLOW.

WAIT FOR US, WE'RE COMING!!

LET'S FORM GROUPS.
WHO KNOWS THIS CAVE?
ME!

THAT'S THE MAIN PASSAGE.
HERE'S THE FIRST FORK, FOLLOWED BY TWO OTHERS, BARELY FOUR YARDS ON EACH SECONDARY PASSAGE.
MY TEAM WILL EXPLORE THE FIRST ONE, THE PHARMACIST'S WILL TAKE THE OTHER ONE.

I BROUGHT LOTS OF CANDLES AND LANTERNS.
WE'LL GO OUT IN TWO FILES, THEN WE'LL DIVIDE IN TWO...AND SO ON.

WE'LL LEAVE MARKS ON THE WALLS.
YES, CAREFULLY. DON'T CONFUSE SWIFTNESS AND HASTE!
CERTAINLY, BUT LET'S GET MOVING! THAT'S MY DAUGHTER IN THERE.

I STUCK MY HEAD IN A LI'L SKUNK HOLE, WELLL...I...

"STUCK MY HEAD IN A LI'L SKUNK HOLE AN' THE LI'L SKUNK SAID,
"WELL BLESS MY SOUL!

"TAKE IT OUT!"

I'M GLAD YOU'VE SLEPT, BECKY. YOU'LL FEEL RESTED.
OH, IT WAS A DREAM.

LET'S GO LOOK FOR A WAY OUT AGAIN.
ALL RIGHT.

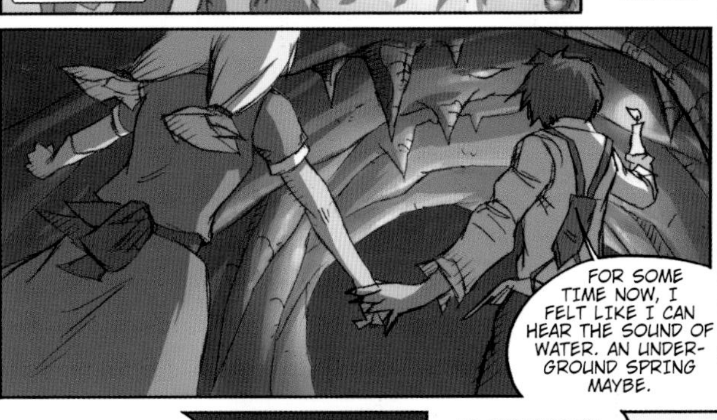
FOR SOME TIME NOW, I FELT LIKE I CAN HEAR THE SOUND OF WATER. AN UNDER-GROUND SPRING MAYBE.

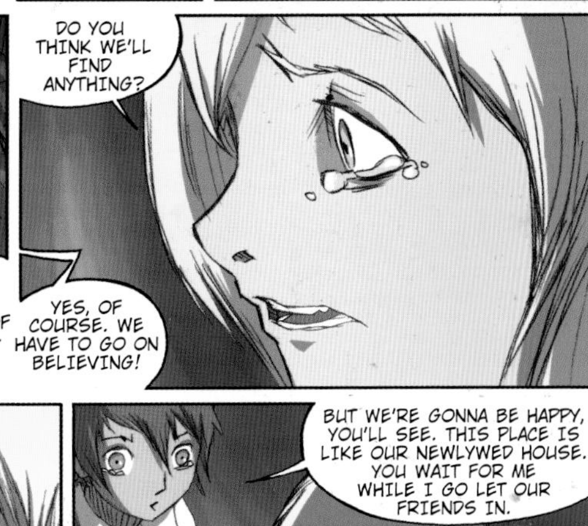
DO YOU THINK WE'LL FIND ANYTHING?
YES, OF COURSE. WE HAVE TO GO ON BELIEVING!

COME, WE'RE GOING TO HAVE A LOVEBIRD'S PICNIC WITH THIS BIT OF CAKE WE HAVE LEFT!

IF I'D KNOWN, I'D HAVE TAKEN MORE.
WE'D HAVE PUT A LITTLE PIECE UNDER OUR PILLOW AND, THE NEXT DAY, WE'D HAVE EATEN IT SO WE'D ALWAYS BE HAPPY.

BUT WE'RE GONNA BE HAPPY, YOU'LL SEE. THIS PLACE IS LIKE OUR NEWLYWED HOUSE. YOU WAIT FOR ME WHILE I GO LET OUR FRIENDS IN.
THEY'RE LATE, AREN'T THEY?
A LITTLE, BUT THEY'RE COMING.
I HOPE MY MAMMA WILL COME FIRST, I'M SO TIRED.

THEY CAME THIS WAY!!

BEEEECKY!
TOOOOOM!

LET'S LOWER THE LIGHT, OTHERWISE THOSE BATS WILL BE RUSHING AT US.
I JUST FOUND A GIRLY THING HERE!
OF COURSE, A BEAUTIFUL RIBBON LIKE THAT WOULD BELONG TO A YOUNG LADY.

WE'RE ON THE RIGHT TRACK, LET'S GO!

YOU DIDN'T FIND ANYBODY. WE'RE GOING TO DIE HERE.
NO, BECKY, DON'T SAY THAT.

TOOOOOM!
SOMEONE'S CALLING US.
BEEEECKY!

LET'S SHOUT, BECKY!
LET'S SHOUT SO THEY HEAR US.
TOOOOM!
BEEECKY!

WE'RE HERE! HEY!
COME FIND US, PLEASE!

TOOOM!
BEECKY!!
IT SEEMS LIKE THE VOICES ARE GETTING FARTHER AWAY.
WE'RE DONE FOR NOW.

NO, TOM, I DIDN'T SEE ANYTHING OTHER THAN THOSE WHISKY KEGS.

TOM, WE HAVE TO DO SOMETHING TO FIND IT AGAIN.
THE POOR CHILD, NOW HE HAS A FEVER.

STAY AT HIS BEDSIDE. I'LL WASH UP AND GO OVER TO MRS. THATCHER'S.
THE GOLD FROM THE TREASURE!

OF COURSE THOSE CHILDREN WEREN'T THINKING RIGHT.
BUT THEY DON'T DESERVE SUCH A FATE.
GOOD EVENING, LADIES. WE STILL HAVE MANY PASSAGES LEFT TO VISIT.

BUT WE'VE ALREADY FOUND THIS.

IT'S THE LAST RELIC I'LL EVER HAVE OF MY DEAR BECKY.

MRS. DOUGLAS, I'M SORRY TO BOTHER YOU AT SUCH A TIME--
BUT I'VE COME TO ASK YOU TO WATCH OVER HUCKLEBERRY FINN.

HE CAME TO MY HOME AND SEEMS VERY ILL. HE'S A GOOD BOY, DESPITE WHAT FOLKS SAY.
GOD IS IN EVERYONE OF US. I DON'T JUDGE IN HIS PLACE.

I MUST RETURN TO THE CAVE, ALL THE PHYSICIANS ARE ON CALL THERE.
AND SINCE YOU WERE A NURSE DURING THE WAR...
I'LL TAKE CARE OF HIM. YOU JUST WORRY ABOUT FINDING THE CHILDREN.

I SHOULD GET A MOVE ON.
I'VE GOT TO DO SOMETHING. THIS JUST AIN'T RIGHT. IT WOULD BE TOO STUPID.
IT'S TOO LATE. WE CAN'T SEE ANYTHING NOW.
WE'RE GOING TO DIE HERE ALL ALONE, IN THE COLD AND DARK.
I'M JUST WAITING TO FALL BACK INTO MY SLEEP TO RETURN TO MY LOVELY DREAMS, WITHOUT REALIZING I'M DYING.
NO, BECKY, NO!
I'M GOING TO SAVE US, YOU'LL SEE.
I STILL HAVE A FEW MATCHES LEFT. I'LL LEAVE SOME WITH YOU IN CASE YOU NEED THEM. I'LL BE RIGHT BACK.
FROOTCH
HMMM...
COME, MY BECKY, BE BRAVE, IT WON'T BE LONG, YOU'LL SEE.
IT'S CERTAIN, TOM, WE'LL SOON BE FREE.
NOT THAT WAY...
THERE'S NO GETTING PAST THIS PITFALL.
THIS WAY MAYBE?
A...
A LIGHT?!
DON'T LOSE SIGHT OF IT.
NO!!

HE BETTER NOT COME THIS WAY, OR I'LL BE DEAD SOONER THAN I'D RECKONED.
WHAT GOT ME A-WANTING TO GO OFF EXPLORING?
IT'S WORSE THAN EVER.
THE ONLY PERSON I CAN FIND IN THIS LABYRINTH IS...
INJUN JOE.
GOD, PLEASE SAVE US. I'LL ALWAYS BE A GOOD BOY FROM NOW ON.
HE'S TURNING BACK.
HE'S GONE, I... I'VE GOT TO ESCAPE.
NO, WAIT, TOM.
IF HE'S IN THERE, IT'S BECAUSE HE GOT IN.
I GOT TO FIND A WAY INTO HIS PASSAGE AND...
MAYBE I'LL FIND A WAY OUT!

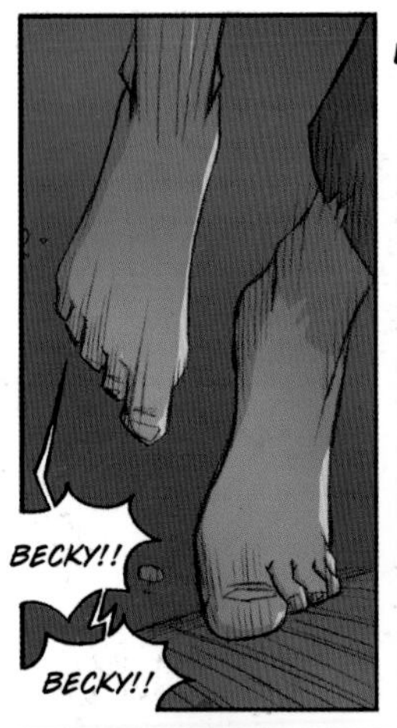
BECKY!!
BECKY!!

WAKE UP, BECK.

I FOUND A WAY OUT!
MMHHHHHH

COME, BECKY, ONE LAST TRY, AND WE'LL MAKE IT.

LOOK, SEE THE LIGHT, BREATHE IN THE FRESH AIR!!
AIN'T IT PRETTY?

WE'RE SAFE!!
YOU HEAR THAT, YOU MISERABLE CAVE?!

?

NOW'S NOT THE TIME TO DIE FROM GETTING CRUSHED!

YOU'LL SEE, WE'LL FIND SOMEONE TO HELP US.

I DON'T WANT SOMEONE TELLING ME HE'S DEAD AGAIN.

TWICE IN SO LITTLE TIME, IT WASN'T TO BE BELIEVED.

BUT ALL THIS TIME SINCE HE DISAPPEARED, WE HAVE TO ACCEPT THE INEVITABLE.

AND START OUR GRIEVING.

I DID LIKE MY BIG BROTHER AFTER ALL...
DING! DING! DING!

DING! DING! DING!
THE VILLAGE BELLS?

DING! DING! DING!
WHAT'S THAT INFERNAL RACKET?!

DING! DING! DING!
IT'S INCREDIBLE!
THAT'S ALL THEY'RE TALKING ABOUT IN TOWN.

DING! DONG!
TOM AND BECKY...
THEY CAME OUT OF THE CAVE ON THEIR OWN.

SOME BOATMEN FOUND 'EM AND TOOK 'EM TO JUDGE THATCHER'S HOUSE.

LET ME THROUGH, I'M THE DOCTOR!

AH, THERE YOU ARE, DOCTOR!
FOLLOW ME. THE CHILDREN ARE UPSTAIRS.

OH, MY LITTLE GIRL, I'M SO HAPPY.
MAMA, I THOUGHT I'D NEVER SEE YOU AGAIN.

EVERYTHING'S FINE, MY FRIENDS, EXCEPT I'M PLUMB WORN OUT.
YAAWWWNNN!

GOOD BOY, LUCKILY THERE'S SOMETHING IN THAT HEAD OF YOURS.
MIS-CHIEVIOS-NESS ALONG WITH CLEV-ERNESS
I DID MY BEST, SIR.

THEY'RE QUITE WEAK AND EXHAUSTED, BUT NOTHING HARMFUL. REST AND GOOD, SOLID MEALS; THAT'S ALL THEY NEED.

TOM!!!

YOU SCAMP, YOU'LL BE THE DEATH OF ME.
BUT I'M SO HAPPY.
I LOVE YOU ALL SO MUCH, I WAS AFRAID TO DIE WITHOUT HAVING TO WIPE MY FACE OFF BECAUSE OF...

I THINK IT'S TIME TO GET SOME SLEEP.

I'M GOING TO NEED SOME HELP GETTING OUR ADVENTURER INTO HIS BED.

I'M TIRED OF THIS, I WANT TO GO FOR A WALK OR GO FISHING.
CERTAINLY NOT! THE DOCTOR SAID THREE WEEKS.
AND IT'S ONLY BEEN TWO WEEKS!

WELL, I'LL JUST GO UP TO MY ROOM THEN.
YOU'RE BECOMING A GOOD BOY. WE'RE ALL PROUD OF YOU!

HOWDY, MA'AM. I CAME TO VISIT MY FRIEND HUCK.
THAT WON'T BE POSSIBLE. HE'S STILL TOO SICK.

OH! NOT EVEN FOR A LITTLE BIT?
COME BACK IN TWO OR THREE DAYS, HE SHOULD BE BETTER.

MAYBE BECKY'S FEELING BETTER.

ALAS NO, SHE'S STILL NOT RECOVERED FROM HER STINT IN THE CAVE.
THERE'S ONE ORDEAL THAT WON'T HAPPEN TO ANYONE ELSE...

BECAUSE I HAD ITS BIG DOOR SHEATHED WITH BOILER IRON AND BLOCKED UP ALL THE OTHER POSSIBLE ENTRANCES!

HE'S AS WHITE AS A SHEET! FETCH A GLASS OF WATER!
WHAT'S THE MATTER, BOY!?

OH, JUDGE, INJUN JOE'S IN THE CAVE!

ONE MORE TURN, AND...
THE DOOR'S STUCK!!
WAIT, I'LL TRY!

NOTHING DOING.
WE'LL HAVE TO LIFT IT OFF ITS HINGES.

HMMPH

AAAHHH!!!

THERE'S NOTHING TO FEAR.
HE'S DEAD.

HE'S CLUTCHING HIS KNIFE LIKE A CASTAWAY HOLDING HIS FLOAT.

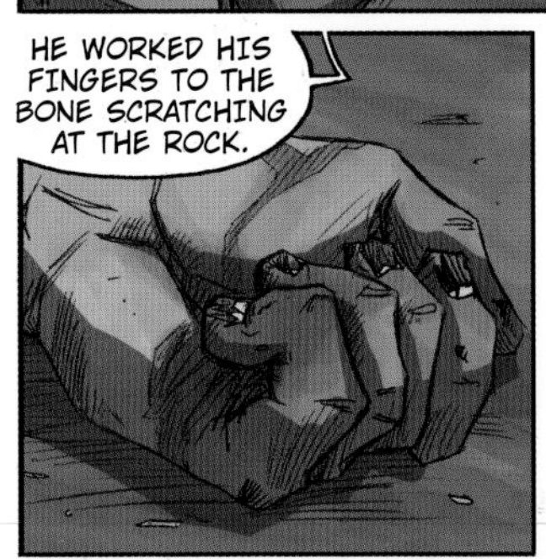
HE WORKED HIS FINGERS TO THE BONE SCRATCHING AT THE ROCK.

HE MUST HAVE EATEN SOME BITS OF CANDLE TO STAVE OFF HIS HUNGER.

RIGHT TILL THE END, HE TRIED EVERY WHICH WAY TO OPEN THE DOOR.

HE MUST HAVE TRIED TO DISLODGE THE BEAM, ALL THE WHILE KNOWING IT WAS USELESS. MAYBE HE WAS ALREADY OVERCOME WITH MADNESS.

UNLESS HE REMAINED CLEAR-HEADED THE WHOLE TIME, IN ORDER TO GIVE HIMSELF A GOAL INSTEAD OF DYING USELESSLY.

THE REMAINS OF HIS FINAL MEALS, NO DOUBT.
OH, HOW HORRIBLE!

AN UNENVIABLE END, EVEN FOR THE COUNTY'S MOST WANTED CRIMINAL.
DEAD, ALL AT ONCE, FROM STAR-VATION, THIRST, AND EXHAUSTION.

MAY GOD HAVE MERCY ON YOUR SOUL, INJUN JOE.

I'M ASHAMED, HUCK.

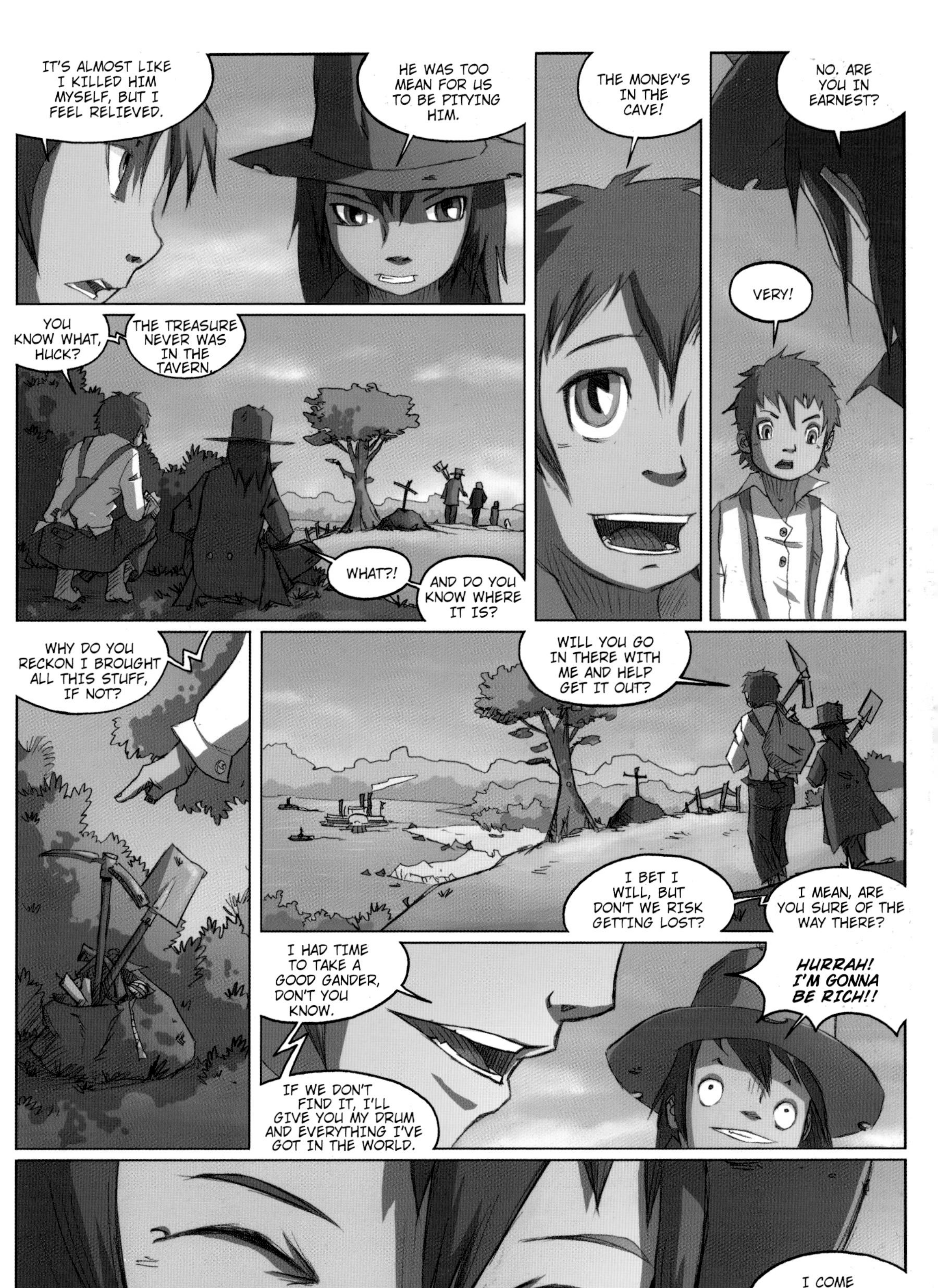
IT'S ALMOST LIKE I KILLED HIM MYSELF, BUT I FEEL RELIEVED.
HE WAS TOO MEAN FOR US TO BE PITYING HIM.
YOU KNOW WHAT, HUCK?
THE TREASURE NEVER WAS IN THE TAVERN.
WHAT?!
AND DO YOU KNOW WHERE IT IS?
THE MONEY'S IN THE CAVE!
NO. ARE YOU IN EARNEST?
VERY!
WHY DO YOU RECKON I BROUGHT ALL THIS STUFF, IF NOT?
WILL YOU GO IN THERE WITH ME AND HELP GET IT OUT?
I BET I WILL, BUT DON'T WE RISK GETTING LOST?
I MEAN, ARE YOU SURE OF THE WAY THERE?
I HAD TIME TO TAKE A GOOD GANDER, DON'T YOU KNOW.
IF WE DON'T FIND IT, I'LL GIVE YOU MY DRUM AND EVERYTHING I'VE GOT IN THE WORLD.
HURRAH! I'M GONNA BE RICH!!
I COME OUT AHEAD EITHER WAY!!

WE'RE ALMOST THERE.

HELP ME UNBLOCK THE ENTRANCE.

ONCE YOU FIT YOUR HEAD IN, IT'LL ALL GO THROUGH.

YOU SEE, HERE'S WHERE BECKY AND I STAYED FOR SO LONG.
THIS SCARES ME A LITTLE!

COME ON, WE'RE STRONGER WITH THE TWO OF US!

NOW FOR THE SERIOUS STUFF, WE HAVE TO STAY CONCENTRATED.
DO... DO YOU RECKON I'LL BE UP TO IT?
POSITIVE! JUST FOLLOW IN MY STEPS.

THAT'S WHERE I SAW INJUN JOE. LUCKILY HE DIDN'T SPOT ME.
TOM, LET'S GET OUT OF HERE! INJUN JOE'S GHOST IS ROUND ABOUT THERE, CERTAIN.

WHAT!? AND LEAVE THE TREASURE?
YES.

WAIT, I'M GONNA SHOW YOU SOME-THING.
A CROSS?

INJUN JOE'S GHOST AIN'T A-GOING TO COME AROUND, WHERE THERE'S A CROSS!
I DIDN'T THINK OF THAT.
IT'S LUCK FOR US, THAT CROSS IS.

IT'S AN AWFUL SNUG PLACE, AIN'T IT? A TRUE LAIR FOR BANDITS, AIN'T IT?!
WE AIN'T HERE A-VIS-ITING.

NOTHING THIS WAY.
HERE NEITHER.

NO LUCK!

LOOKY HERE! THERE'S FOOTPRINTS!

DIG IN!!

YOU TOUCHED SOME-THING!!!!
HRRNN...
HMMPPHH!!!

I DON'T BELIEVE IT.
IT'S TOO GOOD TO BE TRUE!

MY, BUT WE'RE RICH, TOM!
YEAH, YOU SURE CAN SAY THAT!

KEEP LOW, SO WE DON'T GET SPOTTED.

WE'LL HIDE THE MONEY IN THE LOFT OF THE WIDOW'S WOODSHED, WHILE WE WAIT TO FIND ANOTHER HIDING PLACE.
AGREED!

YOU KEEP WATCH. I'LL COME BACK RIGHT AWAY WITH BEN'S WAGON.
MAKE IT QUICK. WE'RE RIGHT NEAR THE WELSHMAN'S HOUSE.

HELLO, WHO'S THAT?
HUCK AND TOM SAWYER.

WELL, BOYS, THEY'RE LOOKING ALL OVER FOR YOU! LET'S HURRY UP.
WHY ARE THEY LOOKING FOR US?
WE AIN'T DONE NOTHING WRONG!

WHERE?
WHO IS?
HAHA, I KNOW! BUT ENOUGH CHATTER, THEY'RE EXPECTING US!

GLING GLING
SO, WHAT'S IN THERE?
OLD METAL.
YES, THAT WE HUNTED UP EVERYWHERE TO SELL.

I'LL HAUL THE WAGON FOR YOU.
THAT'S ALL RIGHT, WE'RE FINE, THANKS.

HERE WE ARE AT THE WIDOW DOUGLAS'S.

I STUMBLED ON HIM AND HUCK RIGHT AT MY DOOR.
LOOK AT THE STATE YOU'RE IN. I'M ASHAMED OF YOU!
YOU KNOW I HAVEN'T DONE NOTHING WRONG, MRS. DOUGLAS. YOU'VE ALWAYS BEEN GOOD FRIENDS TO ME.
HUCK'S REALLY A GOOD FELLOW!

I KNOW. NOW COME WITH ME, BOYS. YOU NEED A GOOD WASHING BEFORE SITTING DOWN TO EAT.

THE WINDOW AIN'T HIGH FROM THE GROUND. WE CAN SNEAK OFF.
THERE'S NOTHING TO BE AFRAID OF. WHY DO YOU WANT TO SNEAK AWAY?

I AIN'T USED TO THAT KIND OF CROWD.
IT AIN'T NOTHING. I'LL TAKE CARE OF YOU.

SO, YOU'RE A REAL GENTLEMAN NOW. THAT'S DIFFERENT THAN YOUR USUAL GRUBBINESS.
RUN ALONG, GREEN-HORN!
POK!
NO, WAIT.

WHAT'S ALL THIS BLOWOUT ABOUT, ANYWAY?
IT'S IN HONOR OF THE WELSHMAN AND HIS SONS WHO HELPED HER OUT OF THE OTHER NIGHT. AND THERE'S...

OLD MR. JONES IS GOING TO TRY TO SPRING SOMETHING ON THE PEOPLE HERE TONIGHT.
WHAT ABOUT?
WELL, WHAT?

ABOUT HUCK TRACKING THE ROBBERS AND SOUNDING THE ALERT!
IT CAN'T BE.
ARE YOU THE ONE WHO TOLD?! YOU'RE THE ONLY ONE WHO'D DO SOMETHING THAT MEAN.

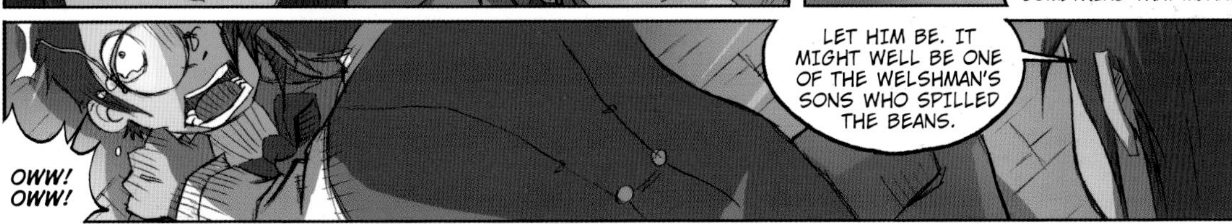
LET HIM BE. IT MIGHT WELL BE ONE OF THE WELSHMAN'S SONS WHO SPILLED THE BEANS.
OWW! OWW!

I'D LIKE TO THANK YOU, DEAR MISSUS, FOR THE HONOR YOU'RE DOING ME AND MY SONS TONIGHT.
BUT IN ALL HONESTY, I'D LIKE TO SHARE IT WITH SOME ONE WHO IS TOO MODEST: HUCKLEBERRY FINN!

?
?
?
?

HUCK, MY BOY! COME CLOSER TO ME.

GO AHEAD!
I'D LIKE TO THANK YOU FOR HAVING RISKED EVERYTHING TO COME TO MY AIDE AND I ASK ALL OF YOU TO SALUTE HIS COURAGE.

SINCE MY DEAR HUSBAND HAS LEFT US BEFORE WE HAD ANY CHILDREN AND SINCE GOD HAS BROUGHT YOU INTO MY LIFE...

I'VE DECIDED TO OPEN HEART AND HEARTH TO YOU AND TO TAKE CARE OF YOU NOW AND IN THE FUTURE.

SMACK!!

HUCK DON'T NEED IT!
HUCK'S GOT MONEY. LOTS OF IT!

OH, YOU NEEDN'T SMILE!
YOU JUST WAIT A MINUTE!

WHAT TRICK IS YOUR BROTHER PLAYING ON US NOW, SID?
NO IDEA.

HALF OF IT'S HUCK'S AND HALF OF IT'S MINE!
OOOO!
OOOO!

HUCK, ARE YOU THERE?

COME ON UP.

YOU SURE SCARED US.
HAVE YOU GONE CRAZY OR WHAT? DISAPPEARING LIKE THAT, WHAT'S GOTTEN INTO YOU?
I COULDN'T TAKE IT ANYMORE. TOO MANY OBLIGATIONS: WASHING, COMBING, DRESSING UP, EATING WITH A FORK, DRINKING FROM A GLASS, SLEEPING IN A BED.

AND EVERY DAY, TOO!
WELL, EVERYBODY DOES THAT WAY.
AND MRS. DOUGLAS IS SO NICE, TOO!

I AIN'T EVERYBODY, AND I CAN'T STAND IT.
AND THE WORST IS WHEN WE'RE OUT AND ABOUT.

WHAT?
CHANCING ON FOLKS WHO DON'T CARE NARY A BIT FOR ME, BUT DO FOR MY MONEY!

IF PUTTING UP WITH THEIR BOWING AND SCRAPING IS WHAT IT MEANS TO BE RICH...

I'D RATHER GIVE UP MY SHARE AND GO BACK TO MY OLD LIFE:
BEING FREE!!
YOU'RE JUST IMAGINING STUFF, EVERYBODY REALLY DOES LIKE YOU.

LOOKY HERE, HUCK, BEING RICH AIN'T GOING TO KEEP ME BACK FROM TURNING ROBBER.
NO! ARE YOU IN DEAD EARNEST?!

YEP, BUT WE CAN'T LET YOU INTO THE GANG IF YOU AIN'T RESPECTABLE, YOU KNOW.

TOM, YOU'RE MY FRIEND. YOU WOULDN'T SHUT ME OUT, WOULD YOU?

NOW THAT YOU HAVE READ THE CLASSICS Illustrated EDITION, DON'T MISS THE ADDED ENJOYMENT OF READING THE ORIGINAL, OBTAINABLE AT YOUR SCHOOL OR PUBLIC LIBRARY

MARK TWAIN

Mark Twain (1835-1910), whose true name was Samuel Langhorne Clemens, spent his childhood in Missouri. At the time of his father's death in 1847, he had varied jobs such as an apprentice typesetter and a steamboat pilot—which leads to his penname: "mark twain!" means "two fathoms by the mark!" that is, the necessary depth for a boat's safe passage. At the beginning of the War of Secession, he enlisted very briefly on the side of the Confederacy before abandoning the conflict in order to go prospect for gold in the West, albeit unsuccessfully. Having become a journalist, he traveled to Europe and to the Holy Land. He would evoke his experiences in *Roughing It* (1862) and *The Innocents Abroad* (1869). Thanks to his two novels, *The Adventures of Tom Sawyer* and *The Adventures of Huckleberry Finn,* Mark Twain found success as a humor writer. He was one of the first writers to use the authentic, colloquial language of the American states of the South and the West. In 1900, he moved to New York and devoted himself to political life, strongly opposing his country's imperialism.

Séverine Lefèbvre

Born in 1977 in Reims, France, Séverine Lefèbvre, from her earliest years, has devoted hours to that which most impassions her: "the game of drawing." Around the age of ten, Japanese cartoons began making her want to tell stories. She therefore created both animals as well as legends, through various techniques, and amused herself by recreating her favorite heroes. In 1993, after completing a high school degree in literature with a specialization in plastic arts, she began illustrating poems, tarot cards, then drawing the first pages of comic strips co-written with a friend. As absorbed as ever with Japanese culture, she was especially taken with the films of Miyazaki. Around the age of 23, she showed her comic pages to Jean David Morvan, who offered to assist her progress in the domain of graphic novels. That is how she came to work at the 510 TTC studio, surrounded by specialists in drawing, coloring, and writing. Her drawing improved, and her first pages were published in *The Chronicles of Wake,* volume 2, in 2005 with Editions Delcourt.

Mark Twain's Adventures of Tom Sawyer is her first full-length graphic novel.